SILENTIS

By

M. Susanne Wiggins

Copyright © 2014, 2016 by M. Susanne Wiggins
Printed in the United States of America.
Cover Art by *Magali Fréchette*
Illustrations by *M. Susanne Wiggins*

ISBN 978-0-9970736-1-4
eBook ISBN 978-0-9970736-2-1

Library of Congress Control Number 2016901075
Data available upon request.

For:
You know who you are.
Not for:
You know who you are.

Chapter One

If they really do exist,
Even Angels would pause to visit:
The Seat of Silentis.

I wasn't planning on killing Christina, but I will if it becomes necessary. She keeps looking at my book bag like she knows what's in it. That's not possible, though. No one knows but me.

Maybe she's just one of those people who notices differences. I usually show up to history class with zero seconds to spare. My book bag normally lives in the land of wherever-the-hell I drop it. Today, I'm five minutes early and set my bag down carefully between my feet under the desk. Her attention makes me nervous and I wonder what she's thinking about when a tiny frown forms on her forehead. She looks up and sees I'm watching her. It's a tense couple of seconds before she turns her head and fixes her gaze to the front of the classroom.

I kind of like how quiet she is, which is probably what earned her the freak label to begin with. But I get it now. There's a lot to be said for keeping your head down and your mouth shut. The quiet ones garner very little attention, except for when they're getting picked on or bullied. When that happens, there's not much you can do about it but suffer through it and hope they get bored with the dead-fish reaction you've perfected.

She's the only other senior who is considered more of an oddball than I am, but I wasn't always like this. Being popular came easy for me until last year, right about the time I walked in on my father and the neighbor, Mrs. Caddo, going at it on our dining room table while my mother was passed out upstairs. The truth is I'd become moody long before then. Having no say about your own future can have that effect. Having a dead brother doesn't help either.

Unlike Christina, I still have enough sway that I don't get picked on—at least not to my face. Instead, everyone prefers to whisper behind my back about how weird I am now. Being from a notoriously ruthless military family is the best protection against assholes and bullies.

Without being too boring or whackadoo with the details, the kind of manifesto I want to create is more like a chronicle of my last day as high school senior. If things actually go my way for once, it will be the end of all my days. I come from a long line of Raynors and upon my graduation, I won't be headed for a prestigious university or a local college of my choosing like the rest of my ecstatic classmates will be.

Instead, it's expected of me to attend an approved military college to begin my potential advancement toward being a Five Star General one day. What do *I* want? It doesn't matter, just like it never mattered for all the men in my family who came before me. If I have interests, they're called hobbies. My preferred career path to be a photojournalist is considered a joke in my grandfather's opinion. Whenever I try showing my work to my father, I get an understanding, yet dismissive, pat on the back.

Where is my mother to defend my rights as an individual? She's lost in a forgetful fog of psychotropic medication mixed with the most expensive Pinot Noir on the shelf. Who could blame her after marrying a Raynor and discovering what life really is like being a female in this family?

Hell, I'm one of the males and even I sneak a few of her pills and hope I meet her on the other side where *this is so much more tolerable than reality*. Sometimes we'll have conversations there in the fog, but I'm never able to recall them precisely the next day.

But every now and again, I do remember bits and pieces of that other side. Like today, and every day since the beginning of my last year in high school. A voice—that I can't be certain is, or isn't, my mother's—tells me to take out who all I can while no one is paying attention to me.

Until a month ago, I ignored the voice. But then the acceptance letter from the Citadel College arrived and suddenly that voice sang out like a bird, urging me to finally listen and do as it said before it's too late. It said I should stop obsessing about the gun I stole from my father and hid away. It's whispering right now, asking me why I keep procrastinating.

When the last student rushes into the classroom, Mr. Scully's teaching assistant, Pippin Montgomery, comes in, shuts the door, and sits down in an extra chair at the side of the teacher's desk.

Pippin is one of last year's graduating seniors and took the assistant job for a year while waiting to get into Juilliard. He was so excited when he got the acceptance letter that he had a copy made on five different colored t-shirts and wore them proudly for a week. His parents named him after the Broadway musical they went to on their first date. Typical yuppie-hipster hybrids.

"Has he said what our final assignment is yet?" Gal turns and asks in a whisper after he settles down in the desk in front of me.

I've known Gal my whole life. He lives at the end of my block and when we were kids, we had *playdates* at least once a week. Our mothers sent us to the same nature camps during summer breaks. We have attended the same schools since kindergarten and whenever we have a class together, he always sits in front of me. I'm as familiar with the back of his well-groomed head as I am of his equally expensive face.

"No," is all I say. I can just make out the slight disapproval in Gal's eyes rolling.

"All right, everyone," Mr. Scully says and looks around the room for errant internet use. "Close your laptops, put away your tablets, and silence your phones."

No problem, I'll turn my phone's voice recorder on. Mr. Scully is old-school. He's probably the only history teacher left in the entire country who still uses a chalkboard.

"Now, Payton."

"Yes, sir," I mumble as I close my laptop.

"Your final assignment is to research one of the numbered subjects on the board behind me and turn in a well-written essay by Friday." His eyes, which look small under his overgrown grey eyebrows, sweep across the room for would-be complainers. When no one dares, he continues, "This is a team assignment." Half the students groan and he smiles. "Teams of five, as usual."

"Can we pick our own teams this time?" Ava asks.

Mr. Scully raises a bushy eyebrow at her and because he doesn't immediately dismiss the request, he has the genuine attention of every student.

"What about the rest of you?" He scans the sea of faces. "You want to pick your own teams?" A resounding chorus of *yes's* makes him chuckle. "If you insist." Mr. Scully's gaze returns to Ava, who's already smiling in victory until he says, "Christina, pick four classmates to be on your team."

All heads turn to Christina. She squirms in her seat and pushes her eyeglasses higher to the bridge of her nose, but avoids direct eye contact with anyone in particular. She glances in my general direction and mumbles my name.

"Speak up, Christina," Mr. Scully says.

"Payton."

"Three more," he prods.

I feel sorry for her. I'm guessing she's worried about being paired with people who are gonna be mean to her. Apparently, Gal sorts this out as well. "Pick me," he whispers to her.

"Gal." Christina leans over a little to see around me and smiles at Sunny. "And Sunny."

"You need one more, Christina."

She eyes the front of the room and there's a shadow of a grin at her lips. "Ava."

Great. I mean, I get it, if she was just nervous about being teamed with all guys. But did it have to be bratty Ava? The one girl in the room whose mother was the one on my dining room table telling my father to fuck her harder.

While Mr. Scully has his fun putting the least popular kids in charge of selecting teammates, I finally take notice of the subjects scrawled in chalk on the board and hope our team doesn't get assigned number three. I'd rather go straight to hell than suffer through a field trip to Joint Base Charleston.

"Is everybody happy with their teams?" Mr. Scully asks, smiling like the cat who ate the canary. "Any questions?"

Yeah, are you Satan?

"Excellent," he says when no one dares to speak up. "Someone from each team needs to come up to my desk and select a number from the box that corresponds with the numbered subjects on the board."

"I'll go," Sunny offers.

Before he reaches Mr. Scully's desk, Jason the Jack-Ass-Jock pushes him out of the way and shoves his giant hand in the box. To my disappointment, Jason waves a sheet of paper with the number five on it: History of Charleston's Architecture. My heart is thumping when Sunny pulls out a number and then the idiot has to chase it down when it flutters to the floor.

When he stands up, I let go of my book bag at seeing the number four: Silentis. It's one of the oldest cemeteries in Charleston, and one of the few remaining that hasn't been bulldozed and built over with posh gentrification. Being a veteran himself, I have no doubts that Mr. Scully hopes we will focus our research on the war memorials. This ought to be a whole ton of not-fun.

Everyone rearranges the desks into stupid circles, and the students on each team can finally look at each other with hard to hide loathing. Some of them are already staring at the clock above the door, or rather the minute hand which we all call the slow key to freedom.

Pippin goes to each team and gives us a list of requirements for the essay, potential resources to be utilized, and hours of operations for each of the subjects' field trip outings. Odd, isn't it? Cemeteries have operating hours.

Another thing Pippin gives when he gets to our circle is a lingering gaze that causes Sunny's cheeks to flush red. There's a hint of a smile on Pippin's lips when Sunny averts his eyes to the closed history textbook sitting in front of him. As I look around our circle, it seems everyone else saw it, too, but no one says anything. Gal gives Pippin a wink before he walks back to Mr. Scully's desk.

Before I look at the sheet Pippin gave us, I notice Ava scowling at me, but she stops when I sneer back at her. It wouldn't surprise me if she knew about her mother and my father. I'm curious, though, does she have problems trying to eat dinner at *her* dining room table?

"Discuss amongst yourselves the timing of your assigned subject's field trip," Mr. Scully instructs before leaving. "I highly suggest you tackle that part of the assignment first and spend the rest of the week working on the additional research and with the majority focused on writing the essay."

I watch him shut the door and I consider how much I don't want there to be a rest of the week. In fact, the whole damn assignment pisses me off. The plans I had didn't include a field trip to a decrepit Victorian cemetery. Then it dawns on me, what a perfect place. I mean, it's not what I had envisioned, but it is somewhat poetic. I can work with that.

"Hello? Payton? Are you here?" Ava's whiny voice snaps me out of my thoughts.

"What?" I bark at her.

Gal intervenes. "Ava said we should go to Silentis today and get it over with. I kind of agree with her because I have a crap-load of prom prep I have to deal with every night this week." He looks at Christina and Sunny. "You guys want to rub some gravestones tonight?"

Christina giggles and I look at her. I don't think I've ever heard her laugh before. It sounds nice. "Okay," she says in a soft voice.

"I did have plans, but I can switch it to tomorrow night," Sunny chimes in, his cheeks flush again after a not so subtle glance in Pippin's direction.

"Well?" Ava asks, glaring pointedly at me.

They look at me like I could be the potential troublemaker. I part ways with my old plans and embrace the new ones forming in my mind. "My schedule's free," I say, shrugging indifferently while staring back at Ava. A memory of her eyes expressing a different look comes to mind and I break eye contact first.

"Shocker," she mutters.

"One condition, though."

"And what is that?" Ava asks.

"It's a history assignment, in one of the oldest cemeteries around." I pick my phone up. It's still recording, but they don't know that. "We turn our cellphones off while we're there."

"Why?"

"Ambiance?" For some reason, I want to strangle her. "Oh, yeah, and we go right after school."

"Actually, that sounds fun. Au natural for the sake of history." Again, Gal puts an end to a potential shouting match between Ava and myself. "We can all go in my car. Mine's bigger." He smiles and bats his eyes. "Meet me in the parking lot after school."

Chapter Two

There is no way I'm going to sit through another two classes before meeting them all by Gal's SUV. I head home during lunch hour and ready my backpack with the items for my new plan. Once I recheck and secure the gun in the hidden pocket of my backpack, I sit down at the desk in my bedroom and write a letter to my mother. Just before hiding it under my pillow, I read it one more time, trying to imagine what the words would seem like to the second most important person in my life.

> *Dear Mom,*
> *Let me start off by saying that I'm*
> *sorry you're having to read this. I*
> *want you to know how much I love*
> *you and how much I think you*
> *deserve better than the kind of life*
> *you're living. After you bury me,*
> *and after you sober up from having*
> *to do it, I want you to leave my*
> *father. Divorce that son of a bitch*
> *and start over again. By the way,*
> *he's fucking Mrs. Caddo.*
> *I'll meet you on the other side.*
> *Always your loving son,*
> *Payton*

* * *

I'm sitting at the porno dining table with my laptop, updating the final moments of my life thus far while ditching my last two classes. The new plan I have now bothers me a little bit.

I've read several manifestos of mass shooters. Some were pathetic, like in the I-was-born-weighing-seven-pounds boring sense. Others were so deranged, I couldn't finish reading them. A common theme was that they wanted to take at least one other person with them before killing themselves.

I know that I don't want to be alive anymore. If the afterlife is anything like where I go when I pop my mother's pills, then it's a lot better than the hell of a military college. Even if there is absolutely nothing at all, it's still better than being a Raynor.

My old plan was to take out a few shitheads at school today before offing myself, particularly the ones who could use a good dose of karma. Several come to mind, and if there is ever any doubt who I had originally considered, just think of what happened at the party after last year's final football game.

I was going to do it this morning, but I overslept and was late for first period. Just when I was wrapping my head around doing it at lunch hour, this crazy history assignment made me rethink things. I refuse to consider that I don't have it in me. It's possible, but I don't want to think about it because that's not part of any plan—the old one, or the new one.

Dammit! It's impossible not to, though.

Gal's never done anything bad, as far as I'm aware, but his lawyer parents are with the same firm who defended the assholes and helped them get away with what they did to those girls. I'm sorry, but a year's expulsion and being banned from ever playing high school or collegiate football again isn't punishment enough. You know what? They don't deserve another word from my life's final account. Moving on.

I have plenty of reasons to take Ava with me. She's been a bitch to me lately for one thing. I've lost count of the times we almost had sex. Technically, I think we sort of did once, but we were drunk and I blacked out. We both agreed at the end of our sophomore year to stop meeting at the tree house in her backyard in the middle of the night. That was also the year my older brother died—the year I died inside.

Somewhere near the start of our junior year, I stopped sneaking the occasional glance through my window blinds into hers. Now that I give it more thought, maybe I stopped wanting Ava in that way when I saw the ass end of my father pounding away at her mother. Thinking further on it, that was also about the time Ava started acting like a bitch.

Sunny and I never hung out in the same circles. I only know what I've heard about him. For all I really know, he's a great guy who just happens to have bad luck.

Christina is the one I have the most trouble with. She has been picked on since transferring here at the beginning of her junior year. After being here for almost two years, and so close to graduation, not one of the assholes at our school has befriended her. Maybe I'll spare her and give her this manifesto to share with everyone after I'm gone. Maybe I'll spare all of them and just go solo. Shit! I want *someone* to go with me. It scares the hell out of me thinking of going alone.

I have to go now, the last class is almost over. I'll have to use the pen microphone and camera to send recorded voice and image updates to my phone since I was the genius who suggested no cellphones. Unfortunately, that was the only thing I could think of that would make them put their phones away during the field trip. I got lucky when Gal sided with me. If it works out, maybe I am a genius.

* * *

"Apparently, I'm the first one here," I grumble into my phone while waiting by Gal's car in the school parking lot. My words display themselves on the screen from the speech to text app I had installed months ago. "How cool is this shit?" I'm watching this question form itself when a voiced echo of it scares the hell out of me.

"How cool is what?" Christina asks from the back of Gal's SUV.

"This app," I answer and show her the words appearing as text.

"I have that, too." Christina pulls out her phone and looks at me for a moment before tapping it against mine.

"Did you just sync your phone to mine?"

"Yeah." She gives me a worried expression, nervous, like she's afraid I'll get mad.

"Cool." For added measure, I nod and grin so she'll relax. Over her shoulder, I see the other three members of our team walking over to us. In a spur of the moment decision, I bring the phone to my lips and say while making eye contact with Christina, "Phone, allow Christina Matthews access."

"I thought you said no cellphones," Ava says to me. She glances at Christina for a moment, then positions herself between us to give me her signature smirk.

"Are we there yet, Ava?" I try to dismiss her by taking a few steps back.

She reclaims those steps toward me and says, "Pendejo."

For a second, I try ignoring her, but I can't help myself. "Chupame la pija, puta."

Her eyes widen and her lips part slightly. Whatever it is she considers saying remains unsaid as she turns away from me to get in the front seat. I feel like a jerk suddenly and go to apologize. "Ava . . ."

"Stop it." Gal prevents me from opening the car door by gripping my elbow and leading me to the open backseat door. "That's enough. Let's go."

Relenting with my own signature move, I shrug, and pile into the back with Christina and Sunny. I'm keenly aware of Christina paying attention to the whereabouts of my phone and how she notices me twirling my pen between my fingers. I had considered pretending like it's a new quirk I've picked up, but under her scrutiny I choose to stick it in my front shirt pocket instead.

Sunny, to my left? Yeah, he just stares out the window and daydreams over whatever gay guys who haven't outed themselves to their parents yet think about.

Gal? Now, he is the coolest gay guy I know, or ever would know if I wanted to live a full life. He is all kind of out and quite proud about it, too. And why not? He's also the smartest guy I know. Even though I hate his parents for being partners in a law firm that would take on rapist clients, I have to admit their awesomeness for having been supportive of Gal's orientation his entire life. And I assure you, Gal has been gay since forever.

With one glance at Ava, I can tell she's still pissed about what I said. Her arms are tightly crossed as though she's performing double duty with the seat belt keeping her in place. She's staring straight ahead at the road that leads us away from Charleston Harbor Preparatory Academy, or as I like calling it, Elitist Shithole High.

I frown at recognizing the most recently city-approved high rise monstrosity. Or rather, I hear the pile driver despite Gal's thumping speakers.

"Hey, you missed the turn to Silentis," I yell over his song selection.

"Calm down, Caulfield." Gal gives me a chastising parental look of warning through the rearview mirror. "I want to stop by my house to get a few things before we go to the mosquito infested cemetery."

"Are your parents home?"

"Hell no." Gal laughs and his gum falls out onto his lap. He lets down the window and almost throws it out. Memories of stepping on hot asphalt-gum must be what guilts him into wadding it up in a tissue instead. "I haven't seen them in weeks. They've been working late every night because they quit the firm and are opening their own. I'm the happy and proud son of parents opening a law firm for civil rights cases only."

Well, there goes the only excuse I had to hate his parents.

Chapter Three

While everyone else is preoccupied with touring Gal's house, I look over the assignment sheet again. It's the operating hours of Silentis I'm interested in rereading and making sure they haven't changed from the last time I was there. I have been in that cemetery loads of times. There's a lot of Raynors buried there. I'm trying really hard not to dwell on the memory of my most recent visit. It was when we buried my brother, Wade.

I swiped the key to our family crypt before I left my house. I've seen the caretaker who works there. He's an old guy with a beer belly and I have no idea if he's bald or not because he always wears a grungy ball cap. All he does is ride around in his beat-up truck shooing everyone out of the cemetery before he closes and locks the front gates.

If I can get my other teammates in the Raynor Mausoleum while the old guy is making his rounds, we'll be stuck there all night. The walls surrounding Silentis are ten feet high for good reason: to keep out kids, vandals, grave robbers (yeah, believe it or not, that still happens), drug dealers, romance, and those who want to fish in the creeks.

I don't trust any of them about not using their cellphones, though. When we're on our way there, I'm going to insist we leave them in Gal's car.

They're stomping down the stairs now and my nerves are getting to me. Nothing a valium can't fix. I brought enough for everyone and I hope they'll take them willingly. Ava will, she knows I nick the low milligram ones from my mom and she has flat out asked me for them before.

"What?" Gal looks at me, wearing that expression he's famous for. It's kind of fatherly, brotherly, and best-friendly all in one look. "You didn't want to join us for the Braxton-Vanderhorst home tour?" He comes from around the bottom stair banister and eyes the back of my laptop. A wicked smile spreads over his eternally blemish-free face. Seriously, how does zitlessness happen with some people? "Payton," Gal's fatherly voice asks, "are you watching porn?"

Smiling back while shutting my laptop, I say, "No, and I've already seen every crevice of your house when we were kids playing hide and seek."

It's true. I half grew up in Gal's house. We know each other well. At least we did until a year or so ago. Not even Gal knows about the stint I did last summer on the ninth floor of Charleston Memorial. Or as I like to call it: The Nutter's Ward.

Everyone thought I was spending a month of my summer break touring West Point. Instead, I was refusing to *talk about my feelings*. When talking *with* me failed, the psychiatrist resorted to talking *at* me. It didn't take me long to notice that my silence only denied me pardon. So that my fruitcake doctor wouldn't figure out what I was doing, I spent two days barking out random emotions. The ones he liked most, he scribbled down in my loony chart. After that, I threw in a few adjectives and the occasional noun. Subtle but emotionally charged verbs in a quiet voice soon followed. What sprang me out? The pronouns. Particularly *I*, along with some tears I worked up. When I went on about my rosy future, I was discharged.

What did I gain from the experience? How to get through the rituals of daily life by faking acceptable emotions for the grownups.

To demonstrate, and to get the sudden focus off of me, I fake-contemplate for a moment. Then I allow my eyes to flit to Sunny before shifting them back to Gal. "I don't remember ever finding you hidden in a closet, though."

Gal sort of glances at Sunny, too, but doesn't say anything other than, "Everyone ready? Ladies, go to the bathroom before we leave." He chuckles at Christina and Ava. "You don't have the parts us guys do to whiz on trees."

While the girls take turns in the bathroom, Gal and Sunny go to the kitchen for water bottles to take with us. There's a crystal candy dish next to a box of lawyer crap on the coffee table, so I help myself and shove a handful in my backpack after I put my laptop away.

Christina comes out first and catches me snagging a few more pieces for my pocket. She just smiles and grabs a few for herself, unwrapping and consuming one right away.

"Yum, raspberry," she says to me.

"Oh . . . yeah," is all I can muster. I despise raspberries.

By the time we leave, everyone has had a hand in the candy dish. On the way to the cemetery I change my mind back and forth a hundred times about my plans to take one or all of them with me. Turns out it is a stressful thing just thinking about taking someone else's life. I can't imagine what it will be like actually doing it.

The whole drive there, they're all laughing more and more while I'm sitting in the backseat quietly freaking out. We finally make it to Silentis' office parking lot and I'm close to exploding. I'll be fine as soon as I get out of the closed-up environment of the backseat. The second I breathe fresh air, a bit of calm returns to my thoughts.

* * *

Years ago, the office used to be located on the cemetery grounds in a centuries-old house built by the original property owner. It also used to be that vehicles were allowed on the grounds, but all that changed when too many tourists started coming in to have a look at all the history. Too many cars on narrow dirt roads no bigger than forest trails, and graveyard road rage inevitably took out a few monuments, putting an end to all vehicular traffic.

The new office and its parking lot are just down the street from the entrance, a short walking distance that doesn't prepare you for how much more walking you'll have to do when you get inside the gate of the 150-acre cemetery.

Everyone, besides myself, stands at the back of Gal's SUV and dumps out the contents of their backpacks into individual piles. They replace textbooks and notebooks from other classes, laptops, and personal items with their history notebooks, a towel each that Gal provided from his house, bug repellant, and water bottles.

Ava uses a pencil to secure her coiled-up hair on top of her head. Then she reaches into her skirt pocket for her cellphone and places it on her pile of backpack belongings.

She folds her arms, taps her foot, and blinks a few times at me. "Your phone?"

Here's the thing with her, she's short and so tiny. Bossiness tends to make her look adorable. I told her that once. Big mistake. Furious Ava is not adorable. When I refused to get out of her tree house, she 'evicted' me. I wore a cast on my arm for a month and a half.

I pull out my old one and place it facedown (so they won't notice the massive crack on the front that rendered it useless) next to the piles of high school senior life.

"Aren't you gonna empty your backpack? I know you have a laptop in there." She rolls her eyes, nowhere near as well as Gal can.

I'm still feeling bad about the way I spoke to her in the school parking lot, so I say without being a complete snot, "I repacked mine during lunch hour. We should probably take pictures while we're here. I brought my camera and we can use my laptop to edit any of the photos if we want."

"But it's still technology."

"True, but we're going to be graded on our essay. You want to turn in our final with pencil drawings?"

Sunny, Gal, and Christina chuckle at this. They're probably imagining Mr. Scully's face—flipping through pages of an essay while trying to ignore the hideous 'art'. It is a funny image and I can't help but smile a little. Ava sees me grinning and mirrors it.

She turns toward the street leading to Silentis' front gate, tossing a, "Fine," in the air.

Chapter Four

We're all halfway to the entrance gate, when I rush ahead of them. I stand in the way of them seeing the sign posting Silentis' hours and excuse my odd behavior with, "As much as I'd rather not, we should probably check out the Raynor Mausoleum later. It's one of the oldest and biggest ones in here."

When they pass by me, I catch back up to the front of the group and lead them away from the entrance and toward the oldest section of the cemetery. All of them keep stopping to read sad epitaphs and I'm getting exponentially more concerned about the time. Silentis closes in a few hours and I'm not all that sure when or where the caretaker starts making his rounds.

An hour passes where I pretend to care about this assignment. They call out names and dates of importance and I jot them down. I do put forth the effort to focus on the task, though. It's the only thing keeping me calm.

My teammates are still so engrossed with reading the headstones that they are oblivious to the other people starting to make their way toward the front of the cemetery.

Most of these people are aware of the closing time because they come to Silentis frequently to bring flowers to ancestors they know nothing about. It's all about the well-known family names they discovered through research that they are *ever so esteemed* to be related to by some fifth cousin twice removed a freaking century and half ago. It's pretentious, it's pointless, and it makes me sick.

I'm nervous and obsessed with keeping my eyes peeled for the caretaker's beat-up red truck, so I can't be bothered with taking pictures. When Gal starts nagging me about it, I hand over my camera and Ava gives me a puzzled look. She and Gal know how much I love my camera.

When we were kids, we used to go on pretend safaris during summer breaks and take pictures of wildlife. Charleston may not have herds of migrating elephants trumpeting their existence through the streets, or lion prides ambushing neighborhood pets, but we had imagination.

Sometimes, too imaginative: boat-tailed grackles and fish crows became our pterodactyls; Mr. Tanner's old, fat, white porch-cat was our Bengal tiger; and the closest match we had to a llama was Ms. Pembroke's black standard poodle. It wasn't until the second safari-summer that I trusted Ava with holding my camera so she could take a picture of a green anole—the elusive Nile crocodile.

"What's the point?" I grumble at her. "I don't think I'll need it at the Citadel."

She doesn't say anything because she knows it's a sore subject for me. Instead, I get an 'understanding' nod before she carries on with jotting down the dates from the headstones Gal's taking pictures of. My watchful vigil extends past the grave markers and massive oak trees and I notice Sunny and Christina have wandered off to the orphaned infants' section. They're bent over to read and take note of the tiny baby crosses.

"Hey, you guys," I call out to them, the last thing I need right now is for our group to become separated. My gaze drifts over to one of the biggest mausoleums on the entire property and it offers the perfect excuse. "Let's go check out the Legare Crypt."

Immediately, Gal is beside me. I see that, not only does he have the strap draped around his neck, he's also clutching my camera to his torso. He's a good friend, always has been. It feels both wrong and reasonable to consider taking him with me.

"Legare?" He stares, eyes bright, at the monolithic building a few yards to our right. "I'm related to the Legares." His voice sounds wondrous and awestruck, true Charlestonian-style when it comes to name-dropping.

"Oh, God . . . not you, too," I mutter.

"Shut up." Gal shoves me a little with his shoulder. "I'm serious, my mother's great-grandfather, Bayard Legare, is entombed in there."

"Really?" This does surprise me. I had no idea Gal was related to the Legares.

The Legare family has dwindled over the last few generations. What is left of them live in the unaffordable historic district of downtown Charleston. Their wealth makes rich brats like us seem more like smudgy-faced paupers. Back in the day, they were social butterflies—the loved and adored kind. These days they keep more to themselves, but play the social-game enough to keep from being labeled as hermits.

"Yeah. Come on, I want to see it." Gal's already snapping pictures and still talking. "I haven't been here since I was in elementary school. All I remember was thinking it was weird to bring flowers to a building."

I tug at Ava's arm to get her away from one of the saddest angel statues in the entire cemetery. It's collapsed over an above-ground tomb and you can't see the angel's face because it's covering its mournful weeping with a hand still clutching a bouquet of lilies. There is this infinite despair about it, like happiness will never exist again because it was sealed inside the tomb.

Unlike the locked door of the Raynor Mausoleum, the Legare one is wide open for all to enter. No doubt, a small price to pay for maintaining their popularity.

While Gal tries zooming the camera to the top of the entry, Sunny reads the inscription aloud, "Remember us. Not with loss and sadness, but with imaginings of what was, what could have been, and forever with what still may be."

Everyone follows in after Gal, except for Christina. She continues staring up at the inscription. "What?" I ask her.

"I wonder what *still may be* we're supposed to imagine."

"Probably the afterlife," I suggest, but I haven't the slightest clue what it's supposed to mean. "Come on, let's go inside."

* * *

The Legare Mausoleum is the biggest above ground burial vault in Silentis. There are a few family members buried beneath and around the outside of the building within the perimeter of the wrought iron fence, but the vast majority are entombed in the walls. Names and dates, one after the other and etched in stone, line the old brick walls from top to bottom.

Stone angels affixed to the granite walls, twin the giant ones gracing the outside entrance and top of the mausoleum. The smaller angels inside all look at and point toward the entrance; their bigger counterparts outside point to the heavens. Every single one them holds a book with, *LEGARE*, etched on the front instead of the usual, *Holy Bible*.

"See here." Gal flattens his hand, palm up, beneath a more recent inscription on the wall. "This was my great-great-grandfather. Good old Bayard Legare." He flourishes his other hand before it with splayed fingers, like an over-zealous game show host.

"Do you even remember him?" I ask.

"No." He drops his hands and folds his arms over his chest. With a sigh, he says, "My mom's been guilt-tripping me into spending more time with granddaddy. I don't mind, per say, but every time I do he keeps shoving this family-tree book thing in my face. It's like a foot thick, for Christ's sake. How am I supposed to read all that in one visit? And he won't let me take it with me because he says he doesn't know if I'm a *loyal descendant* yet. I think he's going senile."

"All you gotta do is show some interest," I said. "That's all the old-farts ever really want. Read a couple of pages each visit and it'll make him happy."

Another sigh, but not as hopeless, then, "I'll give it a try next visit. Thanks."

"Have you made a reservation yet, Gal?" Ava asks and walks over to a section of wall sans inscriptions. "This spot looks available."

Perking up, Gal asks, "Didn't you get the memo? I plan to become immortal."

"Oh, so you don't like this spot," she says, nonplussed. "Perhaps I can interest you in one of the plots still available outside . . . under the grass."

Gal smiles and shakes his head. "I'll be mad as hell about it, but when it's my turn I'll go in the Vanderhorst Mausoleum. What about you?"

Ava snorts at the notion. "I come from a long line of Atheists. We're all cremated and scattered. Unless you're one of the freaks in our family who kept the ashes in a Ming vase that's worth a fortune and then willed it to a smart grand-daughter who flushed the contents down the toilet and sold the vase for three and half million dollars."

Every chin drops in shock, including mine. I have no clue how Ava's family accumulated their wealth. Her father's a small-time politician, but most of his income comes from the Caddo Real Estate Corporation. Mrs. Caddo does nothing professionally. Except maybe extramarital affairs.

"Your mother?" I have to ask.

"Yep." Ava sighs and stares unseeing at one of the angels. "We don't talk about it because my mom doesn't want anyone knowing she ditched grandpa's remains down the sewer system."

It's Gal's laughter that echoes throughout the bricked interior of countless generations of dead people. "I'd have done the same thing, and for even less." Gal rubs his chin thoughtfully. "I'd flush grandpa for ten grand . . . no problem. Three and half million? I'd bake a grandpa cake and eat it, too."

The sound of all our laughter fills the mausoleum. It feels good. I'm glad there's a bit of laughter to be had on my last day.

We spend an hour scouring the walls for interesting historical tidbits on the Legare family. Gal takes several pictures and views them on the digital display before letting anyone else see them. It's obvious he's becoming more impassioned with still photography and witnessing the birth of an interest I have always cherished, awes me.

It occurs to me after I pull out my laptop and show Gal how to edit the pictures he took, and seeing how fascinated he is with the simplicity of coaxing an image to live and breathe, that I can't take him with me. His life will be great and somehow I know it. I can almost feel it.

If I take anyone at all, it will have to be one of the others. Given the idea of what I have in mind for Christina, Ava or Sunny seem more like the doable options at this point.

* * *

While Gal becomes a photo editing hog, and while Sunny and Ava talk about what-the-hell ever, and with Christina scribbling down more birth and death dates, I chance a peek at my cellphone for the time as I had purposefully changed the clock on my laptop earlier. It now reflects an erroneous hour that everyone ignores because obviously it isn't three a.m. when the sun has yet to call it a day.

It's just past 6:30 p.m. The cemetery closed over half an hour ago, but that doesn't mean the caretaker has left yet. He has to make his rounds to ensure all physical bodies of the living are no longer strolling among the dead before locking the impregnable wrought iron gates. The gates won't open again until eight in the morning. That gives me just over thirteen hours to end the Raynor line of successive future terror.

What I want to do is have a look out the entrance to check for the caretaker, but when I look over my shoulder, Christina is standing behind me. I'm worried she saw me squirrel away my cellphone, but she says nothing about it.

I have no idea what's up with her. I'm beginning to wonder why it is she chooses to always stay quiet, because it seems more and more like there's a reason and definitive purpose for her silence.

There almost seems proof of it when she asks, over-benignly if that's possible, "We still have a while before the cemetery closes, right?" It's close to a whisper, but loud enough for the thought to kind of float through the air to influence the others into a false sense of no worries.

"Yeah," is all I say, but I'm staring at her as though she holds the skeleton key to Silentis' entrance gates. For that matter, she may hold the knowledge and key to the exit as well.

A little quieter, she says, "Maybe we should go to your family's Mausoleum next. It's close by, isn't it?" Christina shrugs as though to be indifferent. "I mean, since it's the second oldest burial site in Silentis by only a couple of months, I think we ought to include it in our essay. I've heard it's the largest. Well, below ground anyway."

Makes me curious *how* she came across that information since it's supposed to be a Raynor family secret that only the office personnel knows about. "Yeah," I say again, rid my face of the frown she's starting to mimic, and attempt a joke. "It's only a sarcophagus away."

I watch her walk away to join the other three and then I take the opportunity to look out the entrance. From what I can see, Silentis is devoid of people, save us. Still I keep scanning, searching for the rusty red truck. Thankfully, it's nowhere to be found. I look past the monumental, stone sarcophagus (whose blue blood name I can't recall) and eye the front door of the Raynor Family Mausoleum.

Even the sight of it makes me nauseated. I'd rather skip it, but I can't pass up the opportunity to waste another hour in there. That's an hour just at the ground level alone, the catacombs beneath are an essay all on their own.

Absentmindedly, I take one of the candies from my pocket and pop it in my mouth, forcing myself to resist popping a valium along with it. The dwindling sunlight worries me and I hope they don't pay any attention to it while we're making our way over to the Raynor Mausoleum.

I'm relieved when all I have to do is keep them from dawdling too long by the sarcophagus, whose name I now remember by its blaring letters etched front and center: CALHOUN. How could I forget that?

Supposedly, it's his far-flung descendant entombed there, but legend has it that the great man's (yeah, right!) coffin was secretly moved to the shrine in the middle of the night by drunken family members who feared desecration of his grave in downtown Charleston.

It is a controversial mystery to this day as to whether John C. Calhoun really smirks there under that stone-columned alter, flipping the bird to its previous owner—the unwary sap who married a descendent who happened to own the right name.

Through the Spanish moss cascading down from the oak tree branches, I catch a glimpse of faded red moving along the dirt road heading in our direction. I have no way of knowing if the old geezer saw us and I'm not about to let him ruin my plans, so I hustle everyone to the Raynor entrance.

It's not until we're all inside and the crypt door is shut and locked again do I sigh my relief. To hush their complaints about it being too dark with the door closed, I flip the only mausoleum light-switch on in all of Silentis.

Chapter Five

"Um . . . why is there electricity in here?" Sunny stares at a wall sconce like it's a leprechaun. "And why does it look so much more modern on the inside than it does on the outside?"

"Because that's how Raynors are." My eyes cling to everything, *anything else*, but avoid the most recently etched name on the stone wall that smacks of a military shrine. "We can't even let our dead have any peace."

There is an agonizing moment of awkward silence and I realize it's my fault because I actually said that aloud. Ava and Gal know about my brother, Wade, and how he died. Well, they know he died in car accident. They don't know it's my fault that he lost control of his car, though, so the grievous looks on their faces are born of the typical condolences.

"Don't be so hard on your family," Gal attempts to break the silent gravity.

My gaze travels up to the inscription above a statue of a phoenix rising from the ashes. The words taste like venom as I recite them, "Even death cannot conquer me."

Refusing to allow the somber mood to win, Gal says, "Okay, so Raynors are oddballs. Somebody's got to fill the position, right?"

It works. I laugh, and then so does everyone else. When the chuckles come to an end, there's still a bit of discomfort hanging over us like a black cloud. Sunny, Gal, and Christina set to work by opening their notebooks and writing down names and dates.

Ava is the one who walks over to me. "You okay?"

"It's no big deal. Thanks, though."

She frowns at me. "Yes, it is a big deal. I know how much Wade meant to you."

"I really don't want to talk about him, okay?" I hope she takes the hint. The last thing I want or need right now is Ava's sympathy.

"Okay," she says, but still stands there.

I can't think of a nice way to dismiss her, so I reach into my pocket and give her a handful of the candy. "Share. Don't be like me and hoard the hoarded candy."

A *genuine* smile graces her pretty face, and with her open hand full of red and green, cellophane-wrapped candies, she looks like a little girl anticipating the best Christmas ever. I turn away first, fearing she may say something cute and precious that makes contemplating her departure an impossibility for me.

After a while of quiet note-taking, I scare the hell out of them by opening the underground catacombs. Sunny is the first to jump back as he's closest to the far wall when it opens inward and nudges him out of the way.

"No the fuck way!" Gal's voice echoes down the narrow staircase. "Your family has catacombs? That you can actually walk around in? Like in Romeo and Juliet?"

He's already halfway down the stairs before I can respond, not that I have a witty reply other than to comment about the totality of his gayness. Following Gal's lead goes Ava, Sunny, and then Christina, each of them a bundle of excited energy.

Before joining them, I glance at the skylights and see the orangey-pink color of early evening trying to kick the shit out of daylight. By my estimates, when we finish gawking at the catacomb vaults we'll be as good as trapped in Silentis for the whole night.

Barreling down the oldest corridor, pausing long enough to gasp at this or that marker, Gal finally stops at the end. Pointing at a vault plaque, he blasts, "Died in 1771! Silentis wasn't even around yet. How's that possible?"

Christina steps around him to read the marker. "Obviously, Beauregard Drayton Raynor was reinterred after this place was built." She points to another and frowns. "And so was Captain George Raynor. Hmm, I think he was a pirate originally before retiring and then buying his way into respectable Charleston society."

"Oh, my God." Full-blown disgust forms on Gal's face. "They dug people up just to put them in here?" He looks at me. "You weren't kidding about the no peace for the dead, were you? Let's hope no one opens another cemetery somewhere that outshines Silentis."

"I have terrible news for you, Gal," Christina says. "Raynors weren't the only ones who did that. Lots of families reinterred their ancestors in Silentis when it opened."

Gal shudders in reaction. "Yeah, well . . . it's creepy." He scrutinizes the plaques again. "Hey, Payton, I didn't know you had Drayton connections."

"We don't. The Draytons split from the Raynors a long time ago." I nod toward the vault. "Beau over there was one of the last. What blows my mind is that you're directly related to the Legares and I never knew it."

"It's not *that* direct."

"Close enough."

"Since you're so fascinated, feel free to tag along the next time I visit Gramps. We can sit around the fireplace with hot cocoa and read together."

"No thanks, smartass." I shake my head at the absurd notion. "Besides, he'd throw me out of the house the second he learns I'm a Raynor." Gal cocks his head to one side and gives me a confused look. I guess his mom has better things to do than waste time keeping up with ancient family feuds. "Legares never really cared much for Raynors," I explain.

* * *

We're still in the oldest section of the catacombs and every five minutes or so, someone snickers about a relic name, particularly Ava. "Cornelius Raynor," she mumbles and snorts.

"Why don't you tell everyone about *your* name?" I suggest.

She smirks at me when the others look at her. "Pronounce Ava with a short A, then say my whole name."

"*Ah-va* Caddo?" Sunny tests. "Like guacamole?"

"No, like stupid parents."

"Well, I've got you beat," Sunny says. "Sunny is spelled with a 'u' instead of an 'o' because it's short for Sunshine." We're already chuckling when Sunny holds up a finger. "Wait for it . . . my last name . . . Enroses. Sunshine Enroses."

"I can top that. At least neither of you are named after a fictional planet," Gal chimes in. "My parents were huge Doctor Who fans. Gal is short for Gallifrey, home of the Time Lords."

"God, our parents were such hipsters." Ava tilts her head at Christina. "How'd you get a normal name?"

"I'm adopted and my parents are older, more traditional. Also, my birth mother requested they name me Christina as a condition before she would consent to the adoption. They wanted a baby so bad, they agreed."

"Do you like your adoptive parents?" Gal asks.

"Yeah, they've been great."

"What about your birth par—"

"Never met them," Christina cuts him off, shutting down further discussion of her family, and stares at the stone floor.

Gal grimaces for about a second, then frees himself of embarrassment with a straight face and a compassionate smile. He walks over to her and takes her hands. Instead of saying something warm and cuddly about her good fortune to have been adopted by good people, he says loudly for all to hear, "Payton's father wanted to name him General Patton." He peeks sideways at me to see my reaction and laughs.

"Shut up, Time Lord Gal the Gay."

It's true. If my mother hadn't gotten my father to compromise, I would have been named Patton Raynor, in honor of the great General George Patton. She knew my father well and argued that kids would pick on me and call me 'Pat'. As she hoped, the strategy worked. My father can't have a sissy for a son.

I lead them to the more recent area of the catacombs, but purposefully keep my back turned to my brother's vault. Out of sight doesn't mean out of mind, though, in this instance. He's there, and I know it, and it's stressing me out. The walls of the catacombs seem like they're closing in on me. I'm worried I might lose it and start running up the staircase, so I swallow a valium. Ava sees me and demands one.

Gal must have supernatural hearing because he shouts from the far end of the corridor, "Hey, I like valium, too, assholes." He beelines over to me and holds his hand out. I give him one and he raises his eyebrows, hand still open. "Two more for my friends over there?"

Like I'd trust him to really offer the stash. "Christina, Sunny, you want one?" I call out to them.

"I have my own," Christina answers.

"Sure, why not?" Sunny says.

I put one more in Gal's hand and he calls me a selfish jerk before rejoining the others. While they are busy note-taking and photo-snapping, eventually whispering when they reach Wade's vault, I stare at Levi Raynor, Sr.'s vault.

It's empty, of course. There are some evils that refuse to die. I hate the son of a bitch. My grandfather is Raynor through and through. He doesn't like my dad, his own son, Levi Raynor, Jr., and calls him a pussy every chance he gets. Says he goes too easy on me and that it's more important than ever that he take me in hand since he went and let his first son die and since he doesn't seem to have the balls to keep his wife pregnant with more Raynors.

Levi Sr. is the reason why my father dismissed the idea of me going to college for photojournalism. Though good at being *Raynor indifferent*, my dad doesn't have it in him to be classic *Raynor evil*. We haven't had a five-star general in the family for several generations and it's pissing my grandfather off. Levi also controls the family money and there is no way my dad's Colonel salary could afford our current lifestyle.

48

Wade had just completed his sophomore year at the Citadel when he died. He didn't have what it takes to be a true Raynor either; he wasn't even *Raynor indifferent*. His personality was entirely too gentle and kind, more of a giver than a taker. Wade was liked by all and that was what the old geezer was banking on, thinking military training would toughen up the softer side and that his popularity would catapult him through the ranks.

Why am I so scared? I think I have it in me to be the kind of Raynor that Levi's looking for. I know I do. That's why I don't want to go to the Citadel. What thought terrifies me every day? I have this feeling that it will be the turning point for me.

But I could die, and make sure that doesn't happen. Evil dead is stagnant, potential evil dead is to wax poetic.

"There's not a lot of women in here," Christina says softly enough, but still it snaps me out of my thoughts.

Just not the reality.

"My grandfather once said that decent Raynor men only produce male sperm. And that when the rare female is born, she'd better show her worthiness by producing sons and give them the Raynor name instead of naming them after whoever schmuck she married."

"Sounds like he was a charming fellow."

"*Is*," I correct her, pointing to the plaque on the vault that is noticeably absent a date of death. "He's a lot of things, but never charming. So if you ever see him . . . run."

She circles the impending death year with her finger and taps the center. "I saw you outside of school not so long ago." Christina positions herself between me and Levi's undated death plaque. "I was in the waiting room of Doctor Mead's office when you came out. You didn't see me, though."

My eyes narrow into slits and then I look over at the others to make sure they didn't hear her. They aren't listening to us, so I give Christina my full attention. "Don't say anything about me going to a shrink to them. Got it?"

She breaks eye contact with me and says, "I wasn't planning on it."

Her voice sounds worried, and somewhat submissive. I hate that it makes me feel a little more powerful. Knowing full well it is none of my business, I ask anyway, "Why are you seeing Doctor Mead?"

"Abandonment issues from my birth mother not wanting me." Christina looks back up at me, and though she doesn't ask, it's obvious she's hoping I will tell her why I'm seeing Dr. Mead.

"Issues with my brother's death, my father's affair, being a Raynor, my mom's frequent check-out through the cocktails and pill line, the fact that I can't choose my own career, and . . . oh, yeah, Doctor Mead told me I suffer from borderline depersonalization disorder. I told him he could depersonalize my dick."

Her desperate attempt to keep from laughing shows in her twitching chin. "Go ahead, laugh. I did," I tell her, but she only chuckles softly.

"I'm sorry," she offers.

"Don't be." I lean in a little and whisper, "You should laugh more often. It suits you."

The air between us shifts drastically. Her whole body turns rigid. The only motion is her eyes, shifting left and right, like she's trying to decide which path is quicker to get away from me. Wow. Am I really that revolting?

"I will. We should probably go see some other historic monuments before it gets much later," she says and steps away.

When she leaves to tell the others we're going above ground, I ascend the staircase ahead of them to judge what light is still left outside. There's enough that they probably won't freak out right away. I just hope they don't notice the lack of cemetery visitors.

Chapter Six

To my relief, they don't notice that we have the cemetery to ourselves. As soon as we exit the Raynor Mausoleum, Gal sees the early evening light and digs through his backpack for the bug repellant, passing it around once he sufficiently douses himself. Covered in poison, we make our way over to a family plot that no one could ever ignore unless you lack a soul.

A stone baby carriage adorns the left most side of the plot; a carved infant's face above it. The baby's death mask commands the attention of any and all who pass by, no doubt the intention of the child's mother. Within the stroller is a miniature garden of white and lavender pansies.

"Any of you know French?" Gal asks, but he's looking at me as he points to the inscription. He knows Wade and I were forced to study the language. All Raynors are. Whether or not we have ever set one toe in France, or ever plan to, is irrelevant. Any other language us Raynors may choose to study is considered a hobby, but one that's actually encouraged (the rare exception).

Without the slightest stumble, I recite the French sentiment. "Comme une rose, elle s'est fleurie pour moi, et elle ne vivait plus que les roses fanées d'hier . . . tout fait dans seulement un matin."

Ava gazes at me, wearing a dreamy expression. "That's so beautiful," she says. "Read it again."

"Uh, no," Gal interrupts me before I get two words out. "I speak above average English and B minus high school Spanish, Payton. Forgive my ignorance, but could you translate it? Please?"

I think about the words for a moment and try to come up with the best way to translate the sentiment without losing its intended emotion. "A rose yet bloomed herself, she did for me, and lived no longer than the opened roses of yesterday . . . within the space of a morning."

"Wow. I enjoyed it more in French," Sunny says and plucks a wayward twig from the immortalizing garden.

Nearby, Christina's voice splits the threatening silence, "Je te verrai bientôt mon mari, mon ami. Je t'aime." She is standing over the father's grave, reciting his gravestone inscription and whose wife's headstone lay beside his.

"You studied French, too," I ask her.

"Yeah."

"What did she say?" Ava asks me.

No thought required this time, the sentiment is easy for me to translate. "I will see you soon enough my husband, my friend. I love you."

"They had eight children, but only three made it past childhood." Christina motions toward the other four tiny graves next to the stone cradle. "They were all loved very much. This was a good family."

A few family plots down, we find another slew of babies. Only this time they are not separated individually, save the first born son. The rest had been stacked on top of one another beneath the ground with a single headstone for them all to share eternally. The inscription reads, *'Our Children.'*

"This was not a good family," Christina says and steps away.

As we walk past another family plot full of tiny graves, Sunny half-groans, half-sighs. "Geez, cemeteries are really sad."

"Ya' think?" Ava nudges him. "What about your family? Is there an Enroses plot in here?"

She leans in closer to Sunny and harasses a ladybug on his shoulder until it flies off. I hadn't noticed it before, but he's not that much taller than Ava.

"No. Our family's burial plot is at a Catholic church in Spain."

"So, you'll have to fly across an ocean to reach your final resting place." Ava smiles at him. "That's so epic."

Something resembling a painfully unpleasant reminder passes over Sunny's face. All he says is, "Yeah, I guess."

"Ooh, now here's something you don't find very often in a cemetery." Gal rushes over to an anatomically correct marble statue. "Not only a nude angel, but a *male* nude angel." He gives the statue a proper head to toe appraisal, lingering at the midsection. "Well, hello there, scrumptious. Ava, come over here and let me get a few pictures of you with big boy."

Ava stands next to the statue and grins. Gal lowers the camera and looks at her like she's crazy. "What?" she asks, putting her hands on her hips and a look of indignity on her face.

"Be creative, Ava. You're standing next to Grecian nudity."

"Oh, okay." She's already adjusting her smile suggestively. "You want the erotic look, huh?"

While looking up at the angel's face, Ava wraps her leg around one of the marble legs and runs her hand along its chest. Her skirt inches up to mid-thigh, her knee just below the marble scrotum. A memory of my hand on that thigh flashes in my thoughts and no matter how much I want to stop looking, I can't.

Gal's not impressed. He brings the camera to me and says, "Here, you take over while I help Ava out. If they're any good, we'll call it angelic ménage à trois."

"I thought you didn't know French."

"I know *that* term." He winks at me.

Turns out, Gal does not have a problem touching women. It also turns out that I do have a problem with it. The first thing he does to set the mood—and grate my nerves—is unfasten a few of Ava's shirt buttons, in addition to his own, to show off a bit of their chests. He hikes her skirt higher by rolling up its waistline.

When he removes the pencil from the knot, her wavy brown hair falls halfway down her back. Then, he poses in all sorts of sensual positions with Ava and angel. At one point he stands behind her and leans her forward so that her face is next to the angel's penis.

I almost put a stop to it right then and there, but he turns Ava around and leans her back against the angel's side, just under one of its wings and kisses her while he fondles the angel. When I see Gal's lower half move against Ava's, my irritation turns to rage. It has gone beyond what I can stand any longer and I lower the camera.

"That's enough. Get away from her!" I move in closer and glare at him.

Gal backs away from Ava and frowns at me. "What's wrong with you?"

"Aren't you supposed to be gay?" I can't and don't bother disguising the accusation in my tone.

"I am." He sounds mad at having to defend himself. "I'm also a theater major."

Ava clears her throat while buttoning her shirt. "I have to say, Gal, you're an excellent actor. You even bring your own props." She smiles and points to the front of his pants.

"Whatever." Gal sweeps his hand in the air in front of Ava to indicate her physical totality. "Warm body, I'm a man, and I have an active imagination. It happens all the time on the stage. Only the newbies blush about it."

"So who were you thinking of that got you so aroused?" Ava giggles.

Grinning wickedly first, Gal answers, "I was imagining what Payton would look like naked in a hot, steamy shower. Then I imagined him opening the shower curtain and telling me to get my luscious booty in there with him."

"Stop it," I grumble at him before I turn to Ava. Under my breath, so no one else hears, I say, "Fix your skirt." She's confused and stunned for a moment, but unwinds the waistband anyway without a word. Once the skirt's hemline settles back closer to her knees, I feel better and walk away. But I can still see the memory of her thighs and it's pissing me off.

* * *

It's when we are studying the Civil War monuments dedicated to Confederate soldiers that the auto-timed cemetery lamp posts light up. Sunny is the one who finally broaches the subject of operating hours.

"When do we have to get out of here?"

"Not for a while. Silentis stays open later this time of year," I lie.

They buy it. Everyone goes back to reading the immortalizing headstones of the soldiers who died after volunteering for the infamous lost cause. I, Sunny, and Christina go the solitary way of information gathering, each of us by ourselves at notable headstones and edifices. I keep looking over at Ava and Gal, and when they migrate closer together, I move in and listen to their conversation from behind an obelisk.

"What's up with you and Payton?" I hear Gal asking her.

Do I feel like a creepy asshole for listening in on their conversation? Yeah, of course. I'd like to think I haven't reached full-monster status yet. Am I going to stop like I know I should? Hell no! I am not so deluded that I don't know I'm still a little shit. With my sense of entitlement, I'm staying right here—unless they catch me. Then I'll just have to pretend they interrupted *me* while I was concentrating on our assignment. I scan the names of nearby headstones in case this embarrassing scenario becomes a reality.

"Nothing," Ava answers. I can tell by her tone, one I probably know better than Gal does, that she doesn't like the nosey question.

"That's bullshit." Because of how well I know Gal, his tone is typical of him not letting the matter drop. "You heard him. He was so jealous he accused me of being straight. And by the way, he's never ever done that before."

"Actually, it's the truth. There's nothing going on between me and Payton."

Like I said before, Gal is smart. He recognizes her generic answer. "Oh, okay. I'm not asking the right question, huh? So, did something *ever* go on between you two?"

She surrenders with a sigh. "A little."

"Before or after puberty?"

"Yeah."

"Oh, really?" His voice inches higher with intrigue. "The perks of being next door neighbors, I suppose? Kids growing up next to each other, experimenting and exploring, perhaps?"

"Something like that."

"Did you two ever . . . you know?"

"Sort of."

"Um, how do you *sort of* have sex?" I hear Gal trying to keep his laughter hushed. "I assume you know how sex works, right?"

"Of course I know," Ava blurts out in an equally hushed manner. "We messed around a lot for a long time. One night, we stole a bunch of vodka mini-bottles from my dad's secret stash and we got drunk. We started having sex, but Payton passed out during the middle of it . . . on top of me no less."

"Oh, shit! How insulting," Gal teases. "Did you ever try again? Sober, I mean. Seriously, in defense of all men, we have to balance the booze to bang ratio just right."

"No. It wasn't long after that when we decided to cut it out. Actually, it was Payton who brought it up, like seriously suggesting it. I wasn't going to humiliate myself by protesting, so I agreed. We kind of drifted apart, especially after Wade died. I started dating Daniel last year, but ended it when he went off to college. I have no desire to do the long distance relationship thing with anyone. Ever."

"That's right! I remember Daniel. He was so hot. You have no idea how difficult it was for me to not stare at him in the locker room. Did you guys ever . . . ?"

"All the time."

"Please, tell me someone that gorgeous is good in bed."

"Oh, absolutely, like you don't even want to know. Unfortunately, that was his best attribute. Daniel wasn't the smartest guy. He was sweet, but such a dingdong."

I slip away from the obelisk and their conversation. Though Ava confirmed my thoughts about that night, the last thing I want to hear about is how good the sex was between her and someone else.

Chapter Seven

After meandering closer to the World War I area where Sunny and Christina have moved to, I act like I've been here all along when Gal and Ava join us.

"Does anyone know if there's a bathroom around here?" Ava asks.

Christina comes over. "Yeah." She points to an old white building. "The chapel has one, it's not locked. I just used it a little bit ago. It's clean, but I did see a rat."

Ava grimaces and looks at Gal in askance. He says, "I can't, I have an irrational fear of rodents."

"I'll go with you," I offer to Ava and turn to the others. "There's a ton of information in the American Wars section. I can almost guarantee that Mr. Scully wants to see this in our essay. We'll meet you over there when Ava's done."

On the way there, I say, "Ava, I'm sorry for what I said to you in the school parking lot earlier. I was being a jerk and I shouldn't have spoken to you like that. Forgive me?"

"Yeah." She sort of chuckles and adds, "I shouldn't have taught you that phrase."

She makes me check out the bathroom first in case the rat is still around. I don't see anything, but I take a piss while I'm in here. Once I give Ava the all clear, she goes in and I walk over to a glass-topped table by the far wall and look at old postcards depicting Silentis when it first opened.

One in particular grabs my attention. It's a view of the giant Smith pyramid from the river at high tide. Standing next to it are three women beside a horse-drawn carriage and I wonder if they are Smith's daughters. Everyone who knows about the most audacious monument in Silentis, also knows that Mr. Smith had to wait over two years in the receiving tomb before the pyramid was completed and ready for check-in, or check-out I should say.

It doesn't take Ava long to do her business. Suddenly, she's beside me, looking down at the same postcard. She moves to position herself between me and the table and looks up into my eyes. "I miss us, Payton," she says in this breathy kind of whisper that makes me tingle all over.

Her hands find mine and puts them on those thighs I keep thinking about. They are soft, warm, and inviting—and just like I remember. Once my hands start moving of their own accord, under the skirt and searching higher, she unbuckles my belt and unfastens my shorts. I don't know where she put her underwear while she was in the bathroom, but I'm glad they're not where they had been when they were taunting me during the naked angel photo shoot.

I may have been a chicken-shit all those other times with her, but on this last night of my life, I'm not about to pass up the opportunity to know what it's like.

With my shorts down, enough for what I intend to do, I lift Ava up on the table, kiss her, and fully appreciate what I should have done the first time her legs wrapped around me. It feels glorious and I have no doubt she's climaxing before me. Her legs constrict me into a tighter hold, her body trembles, almost convulsively, and she's moaning to a God she doesn't believe in and it instantly causes my own. What already felt glorious becomes a euphoria that I briefly consider living longer for just to experience again.

Ava rests her forehead against my chest and sighs. "That was fantastic. I really needed that," she says. "Thank you."

I'm not sure what to say. It seems to me I should be thanking her and I tell her as much. She laughs softly and just before she's about to get off the table, I feel it's my responsibility to mention something. "We, I mean *I* didn't use any protection."

"It's okay. I'm on the pill."

Before we leave the chapel, I say to her, "I haven't been with anyone else since . . . well, you know, since that time with you. I'm happy my first *whole* time was with you."

Something soft and beautiful frames her still flushed face. "It makes me happy, too, Payton."

Just like that, her voice isn't bratty to me anymore. It's like it used to sound when we were kids, full of hopeful adventure, filled with the future. Right now, it is everything perfect. I decide that there is no way I'm taking her with me. Someone like Ava needs to stay in this world for as long as it will have her. I hope it keeps her around for a long, long time.

* * *

We waste more time on war memorials. The temporary release from stress I experienced with Ava dwindles when I see Sunny glancing more and more toward the lagoon, where just on the other side is Silentis' entrance. We can't see it from where we are, so he doesn't know the wrought iron gates are closed and have been for hours.

His head turns and his eyes sweep the landscape. I'm pretty sure he's noticing the lack of other visitors now. Before he voices his concerns, I give him something else to focus on.

"I'm curious, Sunny, why do you let everyone think you're straight?"

"What?" He blasts his fake indignity at me.

"You heard me." I sit down on the marble Exedra monument bench and get comfortable, as though nothing else matters at the moment but hearing what Sunny has to say. "Why are you hiding the fact that you're gay from everyone at school?"

Sunny glares at me for a couple of seconds, then his eyes dart to the others as if he expects them to call me out on being a dick. But they also seem interested in hearing what he has to say and prove it by sitting down on the bench with me to wait it out. I guess we all have our inner-dickhead demons guiding us from time to time.

His shoulders slump forward, looking defeated, and he sits down at the farthest end of the monument.

A minute or so passes of us watching Sunny alternate nervous leg bouncing with drumming his fingers on his knees. The fidgeting comes to an abrupt stop and he says, "It's not so much everyone at school I'm worried about as it is my parents. I suppose I'm just putting off the day when they'll hate me."

"Would they really react that badly?" Gal asks.

"Absolutely." Sunny relaxes against the back of the bench and looks up at the sky. "They would rather disown their only son than accept a gay one."

"Maybe, if you introduce them to a support group—"

"No, Gal," Sunny cuts him off. "Not everyone's parents are as understanding as yours are. When my parents find out, I won't have parents anymore."

Refusing to let Sunny wallow in self-pity, Gal butt-scoots down the bench and puts an arm around his shoulder. "Then I'll share my parents with you."

"You really want a closet homosexual for a brother?"

"I hate to break this to you, Sunny, but the only people who don't know you're gay are your parents and maybe a few ignorant kids at school." Gal's face takes on a thoughtful expression. "Besides, if we're brothers then I can ask you if it's really true what they say about Pippin's dick being huge because his dad's black."

"How do you know about me and Pippin?"

"Because of the boner he has every time you both arrive late to history class. Or, maybe it's that I-know-what-you-look-like-naked expression he has every time he looks at you."

"So, you really are going out with Pippin?" Ava asks. "Isn't that supposed to be . . . I don't know, illegal?"

"I'm eighteen, he's nineteen. It's legal."

"But he's a teaching assistant."

"I know, and that's why we keep it a secret, Ava. We've been together since last year, when he was still a senior. We're not gonna stop seeing each other just because he's waiting for his slot at Juilliard."

"Are you planning to go with him?" Christina decides to join the question and answer session that's technically none of our business. I find it curious she asks a question that involves Sunny's future. She doesn't strike me as the future-plans kind of conversationalist.

"Yeah." Finally, Sunny smiles. His eyes light up and reflect a look full of hope and promise. "We already have an apartment leased and waiting for us. After my graduation, we're out of here."

"Sounds wonderful," Gal says. "Before you go, I hope you'll answer my earlier question."

"Yes, Gal," Sunny chuckles, "it's true what they say."

"So what are your plans after graduation, Christina?"

It seems she finds my question amusing. She crosses her legs, props an elbow on one knee, and rests her chin in her hand. She's grinning and frowning at the same time.

"Travel," she answers. Her tone is matter-of-fact, like the plane leaves in twenty minutes.

When Christina doesn't elaborate on her travel plans, I shift my focus to watching Ava rummage through her backpack.

She pulls out one of the candies I'd given her earlier and holds it up in the air in front of her. "Anyone want to trade a strawberry for lemon flavor?"

"I do," Gal says and hands her a lemon drop. After popping the red candy, he studies the wrapper. Then he mumbles something that sounds like, *'Oh, please, no'*. Gal glances at all of us and gets up to take the wrapper to the nearest lamp post. He's laughing and shaking his head when he turns around and comes back to the bench. "Guess what? We've been eating pot candy."

I'm not a hundred percent sure what he means. "What's pot candy?"

"My parents are working on getting marijuana legalized here. Particularly, tetrahydrocannabinol candy for children with cancer. Holy shit! We've been eating my parents' court case exhibits. They're gonna kill me."

"Relax," I tell him. "There was still plenty left."

"That's not the point," he says. "It's not legal *yet*, and we're not cancer kids either."

"I don't see any cops around. Pass me a lemon one."

Chapter Eight

After a long debate about what historical elements should go in our essay and how it should be written, they announce their intention to officially end the field trip and do the rest of the research on the internet. I have no choice but to accept that it's time for them to find out we are trapped in Silentis, so I get up first and start the walk toward the entrance gate.

We're not even there yet, but within sight of it, when I hear Sunny yell, "What the hell? Why's the gate shut?"

As a group, we approach the wrought iron bars. Gal and Sunny test them by yanking and pushing at where the gate sections meet in the center. They don't even wiggle. Sunny reaches his hand through the bars and lifts the padlock. He groans and says, "Not only are the gates locked, but they're chained and locked."

"Is there a caretaker who lives here? Maybe he can let us out." Ava looks around for a building other than the original gatekeeper's house, which is locked of course. It's maintained as a relic for the sole purpose of reflecting a bygone era. Outside the opinions of termites and tourists, the structure serves no other function.

I'm considering telling them the truth about my plans when Christina speaks up, "I saw a small building near the river. It was behind a bunch of trees, not too far from that Smith pyramid, and it kind of looked like a house. If the caretaker is still around, maybe he's there."

"But that's in the older section of Silentis. That's a long walk from here," Sunny says.

"It's our best option at the moment." Gal motions toward the ten foot high walls. "Unless one of you has Spiderman powers." He looks up at the top of the gate. "And this thing is even taller. Twelve feet, at least. We could try climbing it, but if someone falls . . . bones *will* be broken."

It occurs to me that I can put off telling them about my suicide mission for a little while longer. I know the building Christina is referring to and it's only a shed used to store the groundskeepers' equipment. Keeping up with client expectations, it can't look like a storage facility and that's why it was designed to blend in with the centuries-old appearance. Since they don't know that, I jump at the chance to buy myself more time to be comfortable with them.

"Gal's right," I say and shove away from the gate and in toward the bowels of Silentis. "Let's go see if the caretaker is still here."

Ten minutes into our trek, enter the buzzing sounds of the cicadas. There's no sugarcoating what this means—night is coming. It'll be dark soon and we all know it, but don't talk about it. Instead, Gal flips out when an egret suddenly flies in overhead and lands in a nearby tree to roost for the night. Rather than consider the wisdom of what relating the tale may do to the rest of us, he divulges it in a rare moment of stupidity.

"My parents said this place is haunted," he whispers, keeping an eye on the egret, who is now looking down at us from his vantage point. No doubt it's wondering what the hell we're doing here so late. "Especially at night," he adds as though *haunted* wasn't a good enough word to potentially scare the shit out of everyone.

Interesting. Gal's mom won't tell him about old family feud drama, but bullshit ghost stories are acceptable.

Ava slides closer to me. Sunny and Christina move in on Gal. But Gal is already inching his way over to me, and with them in tow, I'm starting to feel like the pied piper.

"Seriously, Gal?" I glower at him. "Why would you say that?" He sees me trying to sneak him a look of 'we shouldn't scare the girls'. He understands immediately and offers me no help at all in the form of instant head-shaking.

"No way," he says, still shaking his head. "Sorry, Payton, but you're gonna be the protector to all of us if we see any ghosts tonight."

"I've heard about that, too. My parents are on Silentis' board of directors. Technically, they're more like curators," Christina admits and there's a bit of fear in her tone.

It's odd to me that Christina hadn't mentioned this before and I start replaying parts of our conversations throughout the day. The only thing that bugs me is her not saying anything about Silentis' hours, or that she didn't correct me when I lied about it. Preferring not to dwell on it, I convince myself she couldn't have known. Why else would she risk getting locked up in a cemetery overnight?

"There's no such thing as ghosts," Ava says, not too sure of herself, I notice.

"No, Ava . . . and everyone else, there is no such thing as ghosts." I can't believe what I'm thinking about saying next. "So let's not go inviting trouble." Yep, I really just said that.

Maybe I'm not so sure either.

Sunny is watching the tendrils of Spanish moss sway in the occasional breeze. "My parents believe in ghosts."

"What?" Gal shouts. "Your parents don't believe in gay people, but they believe in ghosts?"

He stops looking for mossy ghosts and stares at the ground ahead of his footsteps. "I guess," he mumbles. It's hard to gauge what he thinks about that. Regardless, it's really sad.

Clearly, Gal regrets his thoughtless words. I can almost hear the gears turning in his head, trying come up with some inspirational do-over to make both himself and Sunny feel better. The gears come to an abrupt halt as he says with a smile, "Then maybe there's hope for them yet."

Nodding, even grinning a little, Sunny announces, "I'll find out soon enough. I plan to tell them after graduation."

"Will Pippin be there with you when you tell them?"

"Yeah, and his parents, too."

* * *

We're not far from the shed when Gal broaches the subject of ghosts again. However, he's slick about it this time and leads into it by asking Christina about her parents. "So they're on the board of directors, huh? Is that all they do? Or are they full time . . . what did you call it, cemetery curators?"

"The Matthews are in pharmaceuticals. They own all the downtown pharmacies. The only reason they're on Silentis' board of directors is because their parents were, and their parents before them, all the way back to when it first opened."

"Wow! That's a long time." Gal chuckles, then waits a couple of well-planned, subtle seconds, and adds, "I imagine they've heard all sorts of stories about Silentis that few people know about. Do spill all, darling."

"Gal," I try warning.

Unfortunately, Christina seems all too ready to resume ethereal discussions.

"The original architect of Silentis started getting reports of strange sightings from the visitors who came here to bring flowers to the graves of their family members. He talked to them individually and noticed right away that every one of them were the early morning visitors, like pre-dawn and it's still kind of dark outside because they were shopkeepers or had plantations to operate. Apparently, none of the daytime visitors reported seeing anything unusual. He was worried about Silentis' reputation, so he decided to stay overnight and prove that there was nothing for people to worry about."

The rest of Christina's story gets momentarily truncated when we reach the shed. It isn't locked. Who's going to try stealing lawn equipment from a cemetery you can't get it out of? We call out and search everywhere. Nothing, of course. I hadn't expected the caretaker to still be here and I would be shocked if he suddenly came in with a leaf blower.

I ignore the guilt I'm feeling when Gal, Sunny, and Ava keep trying to find some way to communicate with the outside world. The sounds of their frustration with finding nothing and no one starts grating my nerves.

Thankfully, it's Christina who stops them from destroying the caretaker's desk when she plunders through some cabinets and finds working flashlights for all of us. "Please, stop," she says to them. "Even if you do find a contact list, there's no phone in here to call anyone with."

Maybe I was wrong about her seeing me with my phone in the Legare Mausoleum. Alternatively, I'm thinking she's hoping to guilt me into admitting I have one.

Everyone takes a flashlight and we walk back outside. Though it's not necessary yet, Gal turns his on and shines it at the front of the building. "Best looking tool shed I've ever seen. What a complete waste of time."

I tell Gal to stop draining his flashlight batteries and Sunny suggests we walk back to the entrance gate. "I'm hoping someone will drive by so we can tell them we're locked in here and to call someone."

This scenario had crossed my mind when we were by the gate before. I'm not terribly worried about it since Silentis isn't on a main road. Only the lost or misinformed tourist, or a car full of degenerates, would drive down the little-known road after hours. On a Monday night, that possibility is highly unlikely.

Not to mention we're approaching high tide—and it's a king tide, too. If it rains, the only road leading to Silentis will be a waterway. You would have to swim, kayak, or paddleboard in.

"So what did Silentis' architect find out?" Gal prods Christina.

"The story goes that he was all excited the next morning, but wouldn't tell anyone about his overnight stay until he had a chance to investigate some more. A few days later, he stayed overnight again, and the next morning he wasn't of the same mind. The only conclusion he would give was that it had been peoples' overworked imaginations. Then he ordered the original five-foot wall to be doubled in height, and that a caretaker be hired to lock the newly constructed front gate at night. After he saw its completion, he recommended to the board that they ban visitors when it's dark. Then, he left and never came back. His family plot is still empty to this day. He actually put it in his will as a condition of inheritance that he not be buried here."

"That doesn't sound good," Ava says. "What do you think freaked him out?"

"The first caretaker used to live in the gatekeeper's house, it's that locked building by the front gate. He quit after a week. So did the next three caretakers. The last one, the only one who gave a reason for his resignation, said the cemetery was full of ghosts at night and recommended the board just lock the gates at closing time and leave the dead to haunt their eternal home in peace."

"Sounds like you know a lot about Silentis' history, Christina." It's all I can do to keep the accusation from my tone. "You could have written this essay all on your own."

"But that's not the assignment, is it, Payton? I believe it's supposed to be a *team* effort." She had no such design to hide anything; particularly, the accusation from her own voice. "Are you suggesting that I do everyone's homework for them?"

Where is her gumption when all the shitheads at school tease her, I can't help but wonder. "You should speak up for yourself more often. Tenacity also suits you."

She wants to say something. Her lips are perched on the edge of almost saying it, but she doesn't. Instead, she averts her eyes to the path in front of us, the one that is becoming harder to make out.

Gal won't let the talk of ghosts rest. "The story my parents told me was that the ghosts of some of the people buried here roam at night. Supposedly, they don't interact with the living. Rather, they reenact pieces of their own lives before they died. By morning's first light, they're gone again."

"Cut it out, Gal," I try warning him again.

"I'm not saying I believe in it," he defends himself. "I'm just telling everyone what I heard from my parents . . . what they heard from their parents . . . and so forth."

We get back to the front gate and watch the last bit of daylight leave while sitting on the steps of the old gatekeeper's house.

Hunger hits us all at once and we eat the protein bars that Gal and I had thought to stuff into our backpacks. We hover around Christina while she refills her water bottle from a spigot on the side of the house. Rather than move out of the way, she holds her hand up and refills ours for us.

The whole time, not one car drives by.

Eventually, Sunny says, "I have to go to the bathroom."

"So do I," Gal says and looks down the pathway running alongside the wall of Silentis. "I think those oak trees are available. Come on—"

"Actually, I need to use a *real* bathroom. The kind with toilet paper," Sunny clarifies.

Christina stands up. "I have to go, too. We can go to the chapel." She glances at Sunny. "And I'd like to go first, please."

"Probably a good idea. I had a spicy black bean burrito at lunch."

"That's been you? Damn, Sunny." Gal's nostrils flare. "I was convinced somebody wasn't buried deep enough somewhere in here."

I'm a little concerned about letting them leave on their own, but I relax at realizing the only possible chance of them getting out is by standing vigil at the front gate and flagging down a passerby if one happens along. I still haven't come up with a plan if that does happen. At the moment, I'm thinking I'll just go off on my own and do what I came here to do.

"Okay, we'll stay here. Oh, wait," I turn to Ava, "do you need to go, too?"

80

"No, I'm good."

She tries not to smile, but a tiny one betrays her and curves the corners of her lips a little. It's pretty and I like the way it looks, especially with the pink forming on her cheeks.

I have a pretty good idea what she's thinking about, or rather, trying not to think about so that no one else notices.

To keep them from paying attention to her, I tell the others, "Be careful and remember which way you're going so you don't get lost."

Chapter Nine

When they leave, Ava and I sit down on the steps. We haven't acknowledged what happened at the chapel in any appreciable way. I've wanted to, maybe hold her hand or something like that.

Honestly? I want to do more than just hold her hand. But the interlacing of fingers while doing mundane things like walking seems like a nice experience I wouldn't mind having with her. Unfortunately, we didn't discuss the matter of whether or not we cared what the others thought, or if they should know. And suddenly I'm starting to feel like an over-thinking idiot.

Finally, I ask, but not the burning question, "I might have missed a granola bar at the bottom of my backpack. You still hungry?"

"You're so bad," Ava says, smiling as though she had heard all my goofy thoughts. "No, I'm fine. Save it for later in case we're stuck here all night." She gets up and starts walking toward the side of the house, pausing to look at me before turning the corner.

"Where are you going?" I ask her.

"Got any more of that candy?"

I pull one out of my pocket. "Here. I don't have any lemon drops, though."

"I wasn't talking about *that* candy," she says and disappears around the corner.

I'm frowning, mostly because I can't see her anymore, and then it dawns on me what she meant. I certainly hope so because I'm up and off the step like it's spontaneously bursting into flames under my ass, and trot after her.

If how I translated her comment is correct, then I have no worries. I've got plenty enough of that sort of candy left and will happily give her however much she wants.

Ava is already spreading out the towel in a grassy area behind the house when I find her. I drop my backpack on the ground and pull off my t-shirt—I want to feel her bare skin against mine. She giggles and says something about how pale I am.

I don't know if it's due to my own perceived notion that this is my last night on Earth, or if the sex is really that good, but the second time with Ava in one night is even better than the first. I'm rock hard again, ready for a third go from just looking down at her (I insisted she allow me to remove every scrap of clothing from her body), but we hear the others coming back and that puts an end to reentry.

Taking clothes off quickly is so much easier than putting them back on in the same hurry. I don't know which is worse, trying to hide my erection, or trying to keep the pain it's causing me from showing on my face.

It doesn't matter. A full erection can be hidden with a well-draped towel, but hastily placed clothes and flushed faces tell their own tales.

Our guilty as charged expressions meet them at the front of the house. Of course, it's Gal who notices right away—really, can he smell sex?—and he grins at us. I can see the formation of the many things he would like to say evolve on his face, so I raise an eyebrow at him in warning. Unfortunately, this is Gal, and he finds it hard to resist leaving these kinds of moments unaccounted for.

He settles on, "So, did you guys see anybody drive by while you were behind the gatekeeper's house?"

"Nope, not a single headlight," Ava answers and scowls at Gal. She surprises me by sighing loudly and saying, "Since there's a good chance we're stuck here for a while, let's do some more looking around. Just because we managed to get ourselves locked inside Silentis doesn't mean Mr. Scully will give us perfect grades."

With that, Ava is off to the nearest family plot and I'm following after her like a hungry dog and she's got the bacon tucked in her pocket.

Why does it bother me to see her so easily walk away? Why does it bother me that I care whether or not it's easy for her? If only this erection would go away, maybe I'll stop wanting her to want nothing more than to be underneath me again.

* * *

The five of us are several monuments down from the initial family plot that Ava first went to. We have every one of our flashlight beams pointed at the faded tombstone inscription because it's under an old oak tree that is blocking out the moonlight and lamp post light.

A century and a half's worth of weathering and generous amounts of lichen growth has also wreaked havoc on what probably was a heartfelt countenance of Mrs. Manigault's life and death.

We argue back and forth over what the few legible words are until a faint lilting sound silences us. There is a discernible musical quality to it and we look at each other hoping one of us has an explanation.

"Please tell me you guys hear that, too," Sunny's lips say while the rest of him remains frozen in place.

"I hear it." Gal sweeps his flashlight beam across our immediate surroundings, but he won't linger on any one place for long. "The ice-cream truck . . . I hope. Or a foodie trying to make a retro comeback of artisan desserts on wheels."

Though it's the least likely of possible explanations, I know what he means. There is something vaguely familiar about the tune. It's eerie, too, and sends a shiver down my spine (stubborn erection gone and forgotten). Closing my eyes, I strain to listen and try to make out which direction it is coming from.

Strangely enough, and I hope it's the pot candy skewing my auditory perception, I keep going back to the same area—that family plot with the stone baby carriage.

When I open my eyes, they're all staring me like I found an explanation written somewhere on the inside of my eyelids. I'm not sure what to say, so I shrug and offer a lie, "It's probably coming off a boat from the river."

"Bullshit."

"It was a potential explanation, Gal." Actually, that part is true. Sometimes, music or conversations coming from boats on the water sound directionally odd to people on nearby land.

The lullaby stops, but only for a moment, and then starts all over again exactly the same way.

"That's coming from somewhere inside Silentis," Gal says in a fervent whisper. "Sorry I spit on you." He wipes my cheek with the towel still draped over my shoulder. Even with the weirdness of the music still carrying on, Gal can't help himself. Barely audible, he leans closer and says while pointing, "Oops, now you have a bit of cum just there."

"Cut it out," I tell him and yank the towel back.

Christina eases over to the entrance of the fenced-in Connor family plot, but doesn't go in. She tilts her head as though trying to sort out the direction of the sound for herself.

"It's coming from the other side of the lagoon." She looks over at us. "We were there earlier. Remember, the White's family plot? The one with all the French writing on the headstones."

"The one with all the babies?" Sunny asks.

"Sunny, most of the older sites had a lot of babies," Ava says and goes to stand by Christina. "The Whites are the ones with the stone baby carriage, right?"

"Yeah."

"Maybe their descendants are eccentric and put a speaker in the plot as a memorial," Gal suggests. "Anyone want to go check it out?" The lack of conviction in his voice hints at what he hopes we'll say.

"I kind of do," Ava says.

Sunny sighs. "Me, too. Not knowing will haunt me more than a ghost ever could."

"I'm up for it." Christina's eyes flash to me and Gal. "What about you two?"

"Fine," I grumble.

"Well, I'd rather not. But I'm certainly not staying here all by myself." Gal's nostrils flare his displeasure at either option. "I guess I *have* to go."

"Don't worry," I say. "If it's a haunted speaker, I'll protect you."

* * *

While we're crossing the bridge that spans the lagoon, I point my flashlight beam over the water and spot several sets of glowing eyes watching us. "No swimming for us tonight," I tell them.

"Are those—?" Christina can't quite finish her horrified question.

"Alligators!" Sunny shrieks and one set of eyes sinks below the water. He gasps his obvious fear when they don't reemerge.

Gal, Ava, and me just look at each other and shrug. Alligators are everywhere in and around Charleston. Maybe not prowling the streets like thugs, but you don't need to travel far to see them. The ones not sitting on your dinner plate in the form of gator bites or gator sausage, you simply keep a respectful distance from. That's all you need to know about alligators.

After reassuring Christina and Sunny that they aren't hunting us, we continue moving along the bridge. By the time we reach the other side of the lagoon, the music stops abruptly. This time, it doesn't start up again right away.

We're all standing here at the base of the bridge, not talking, and not planning—only waiting for something to happen. At the very least, we are each wondering if one of us—but not ourselves—will offer a suggestion. Finally, I'm the one who puts an end to the weenie-gang meeting.

"Come on." I start walking. "So what if it stopped? We already have an idea where the sound was coming from."

Even with the soft glow of the lamp post lights and the beams from our flashlights, it is still difficult to navigate the massive cemetery in the dark. It's almost like a foreign world, so different from the one existing under the sun.

Proof of that comes when Christina says, "We've been going the wrong way. I remember now, it's closer to the widest part of the lagoon."

We turn around and retrace our steps back to the bridge's base from memory with flashlights off to conserve their batteries. This whole time, the music still hasn't started up again.

"All right," Christina mutters from the front of our single-file line and turns on her flashlight. The beam of light falls on the stone carriage, but all we see is how white and lavender flowers look at night. They look the same as during the day, if any horticulturists are ever curious.

Her flashlight flickers a few times and then completely cuts out. After shaking and hitting it against her palm, to no avail, she utters her first expletive remark (that I've heard anyway), "Dammit! I think the batteries just died."

The music starts again and the dead batteries of Christina's flashlight fall to unimportance as her head lifts slowly, looking to us first, then to whatever must be lurking behind us. There's no need for her to say a word, the rest of us reel back to see what Christina is staring wide-eyed at. I imagine, if I could tear my gaze away from the strange entity, I would see similar slack-jawed individuals standing next to me.

The sound is coming from the entity, who's humming the lullaby and now gliding (or floating, it's hard to tell if this thing has feet when you're trying not to scream) over to the carriage.

It, I suppose it's Mother White, pauses her humming to smile down at an infant that to us is a stone basin of flowers. She says in what seems more like a verbalized thought, "Hush now. No more of that coughing from you, little Rosalie."

She continues on with her humming, but stops again at what we all perceive is a knock at a door that only exists in this woman's world. Her features become taut with conflict and dread before she starts moving toward the unseen door.

Here's what I'm seeing; this thing isn't white like you would imagine, but rather it's dark like everything else around it because of the darkness of night. Also, there's a shimmering quality to it, not unlike that weird look on a road in the distance ahead of you on a blazing hot day but with less rippling. Yet it is nighttime, so it takes on a kind of spookiness that demands your attention and forces every hair on your body to stand on the tip of a goose bump.

It reminds me of a creature I saw in a movie once. That movie scared the shit out of me, and so does what I'm looking at right now.

Unfortunately, Mrs. White passes through Christina on her way to the *door*. And for the already strange to downgrade to unacceptable freakish horror, all it takes to disrupt a replaying spectral memory is to pass through a living being who yells, "Holy Shit!" at the way it must feel.

Mrs. White ignores answering the door to address this new, *holy-shit* situation. There is no denying it, she's making direct eye contact with Christina and demands, "Who are you? And how did you get in Rosalie's nursery?"

I can't tell if Christina is about to faint or scream. By the look on her face, she doesn't seem to know which one either. "Uh . . . I, I mean, we," she stammers, ". . . heard music?"

Screaming, fainting, or lack of witty answers become a moot point. As soon as the stammering words pass Christina's lips, Mrs. White screams, "DID YOU KILL MY BABY?"

Only now is there a bit of the white light you would expect from a stereotypical ghost. It forms from a small point at the center of the dark shimmering quality of the entity and explodes in a fantastic light that sends us all running in different directions.

Maybe not *all* of us. I do run, but keep my sight zeroed in on Ava. If I weren't so busy being scared out of my mind, I would be impressed with how fast she can run. Dust is actually billowing up behind her!

When I catch up, I grab her arm mid-stride and drag her along with me and race us toward no preplanned destination in particular. We hurtle past several trees that are big enough to hide behind, but I'd rather put more distance between us and whatever that thing is. I spot a wide oak up ahead near a lamp post and head for it.

We cower behind four or five hundred years of tree growth, out of breath, and take occasional peeks around the enormous trunk. I imagine we look like those squirrels you see clinging to tree trunks upside down and they keep scurrying to the other side in that *you-must-not-see-me* thing they do.

"Think the others got away?" Ava asks in a whisper, still panting.

"I hope so."

The event provides me with a glimpse into myself that I hadn't been aware of before. We all scattered at the same time, self-preservation being top priority.

Of the five of us, I'm the only who chose to ensure the safety of another—Ava. I'm not all that surprised that Sunny and Christina didn't rank on my list of who I value most, but I've known Gal my whole life and I feel bad for not knowing where he is now.

I'm not sure what possesses me to do it after a minute or so of seeing and hearing nothing unusual. Maybe it's the way she looks so fearful and vulnerable in the soft glow of the nearby lamp post, or perhaps it's because we had sex twice tonight, that makes me feel entitled when I cup Ava's face in my hands and kiss her.

She responds favorably for a bit before she struggles against it. I'm not bothered or surprised by it, I'm just glad she kissed me back first.

"What the hell just happened back there?" Ava asks and chances another peek around the tree trunk. She turns and looks back up at me. "What's happening, Payton?"

Damn if I don't want to kiss her again. Desire is rarely rational.

The inability to come up with an explanation clears my head. "I don't know. I'd like to blame it on hallucinations from eating that candy, but that doesn't seem likely if we're all experiencing the same thing."

"We should go look for them," she puts forward as if it is the right thing to say at this juncture. But I can hear the unspoken suggestion in her tone: *'Want to find somewhere to hide with me till morning?'*

I stand up first, then help her to her feet. "Yeah, we should find them," I dash her secret hopes.

Chapter Ten

We find Sunny first. He's already out from wherever he hid and is looking around for the rest of us. It's understood between the three of us that we're not going to talk about what happened until we are all together again.

It's Gal's voice calling out to us that we hear next before actually seeing his form, which is darting from tree to tree and waiting a good minute before verbalizing his presence.

Similarly, we find Christina by way of voice. The difference is that she had scrambled up one of the oak tree trunks that leans over enough to produce a kind of ramp to its innards. She sees us first and whispers loudly (what's the point of a loud whisper?), "I'm up here." Christina refuses to budge from her position, so we climb up to join her.

"You okay?" I ask her when we all find suitable seats in the tree.

"Not really," she answers, the words pass by two pieces of pot candy she had popped into her mouth. "It's not every day I get accused of killing a baby by a . . . a whatever the hell that thing was."

"Technically, she didn't *accuse* you, she only asked if you had killed her baby."

Christina looks at Gal like he's stupid. She takes a deep breath as if to calm herself, and probably to keep herself from yelling at him. "I've been hiding up here since I ran off." While pointing at the White's family plot, which we can see clearly from our darkened vantage point, she continues, "There hasn't been any more music, and I haven't seen that dark figure again."

"Though I think there has to be a logical explanation for what we saw, I'm gonna go out on a hypothetical limb here." Sunny tugs on a piece of Spanish moss and twirls it around his finger. Either he is reluctant to voice his ideas, or he's trying to piece them together as they form. "*If* that was a ghost, like the kind Gal mentioned earlier, then I'm thinking we may have somehow done something that interrupted its normal routine. Maybe that's why it seemed like Mrs. White suddenly joined the *now*, instead of staying in her *then*."

Not that I believe this shit but I offer a follow-up explanation, because it is impossible to not get caught up in a conversation that involves hypothetic ghosts while sitting in a tree. "And maybe when she stepped out of her typical haunt, it caused that explosion of light and stopped it from replaying again."

We stop talking to watch and listen. All is still quiet with no sign of movement by the stone carriage.

There's a boatload of thoughts running through my head, worrying me, giving me crap to stress over that I hadn't planned on having to deal with. What if this ghost business isn't bullshit after all? If that's the case then I have a ton of questions, with no real way of finding the answers, and a strong desire to stay far away from the Raynor Mausoleum.

"What's the plan?" Gal asks. "We can't sit up here all night."

Ava shoots him a disapproving glare. "Why not? Here's good."

"We should make our way back to the front gate," Gal says. "We could very well be stuck here till morning and I don't want to wait the night out in a tree. If we fell asleep up here, someone could fall and I'd rather not have to deal with injuries on top of everything else."

"Gal's right," Christina says as she stands up. "Let's go back to the front gate."

Ava is the last one down out of the tree and announces, somewhat apologetically, "I have to pee."

Unfortunately, so do I, but I'm not gonna ask her to squat and pee by a tree that I'm pissing on. The thought of how much ground we will have to cover just to get to the bathroom in the chapel kind of freaks me out. I strategize a plan and hope it works out for the best.

"We'll all go to the chapel together and everybody should take care of their business, whether you have to go or not." I scan the family plots surrounding us and see nothing. I shush them so we can listen and all we hear are the songs of tree frogs. "Also, if we see or hear anything, let's just ignore it and keep walking."

"I agree," Sunny says. "And I'd add that we don't talk to them either."

"Or let one walk through you," Christina mutters. "That felt all kind of wrong, you have no idea."

I turn around and nearly run into this headstone I've seen more times than what should be allowed in one lifetime.

"You want to see something really depressing?" I ask.

"No," Gal answers, for everyone apparently.

"Too bad. Look anyway." I shine the flashlight on the hideous inscription from 1861 and read it aloud in case they're choosing to ignore it. "Husband and father. Kind and affectionate. Indulgent Master. Just and generous to all."

"Damn," Gal says. "That's messed up."

"Yeah, I'm calling bullshit on the just and generous part," Ava says.

Sunny shines a light on a nearby headstone. "Look, here's another one. A kind and just Master. A sincere and consistent Christian." He shakes his head. "There is nothing Christian about that."

* * *

As I have already mentioned, it's difficult (close to impossible) to navigate through such a vast area in the dark. The headstones lose their individuality, unless they're one of the head-turners that triggers the mental map in one's head.

It's that damn pyramid we all but bump into, telling us we managed to miss the chapel thanks to Gal's suggestion that we take a straight line rather than follow along the roads.

Before we turn to head away from the monument, we hear a young female's voice say, "Father would have loved it."

Defying our agreement, I glance over my shoulder and find the three women I'd seen earlier on the postcard at the chapel. So does Ava.

Like Mrs. White, they have the same dark form. The difference between the scene on the postcard and what Ava and I are witnessing, is that they aren't standing by a horse drawn carriage. They have moved to the back of the pyramid to admire the stained glass mural—not even five feet away from us.

Ava is so terrified, I don't think she is breathing out of fear of it being overheard.

Slowly, I reach for her shaking hand when I see one of the women backing up to take in a fuller view of the mural. The Smith daughter must have tripped on the infant's headstone originally, as she is also doing in the replaying memory, falling right down the center of my and Ava's joined hands.

The instinctive reaction would be to gasp, and that is exactly what Ava and I both do.

The woman, reposed on her backside, instantly looks up at us. "What is this? Have I died?" she asks us.

Her eyes scan Ava's clothing. "Certainly not, I'd say. Unless heaven is a brothel."

The other two sisters come over to help their fallen sibling. They, too, eye Ava with obvious disdain. "Oh, dear," one says and casts a judgmental look in my general direction. "Sir, please take your whore somewhere else."

"*Whore*? You fucking self-righteous bitches," Ava shrieks. "How dare you call me a whore?"

As soon as I see that same light beginning to form, this time a trio of them, I turn with Ava and run. We catch up to and then surpass Gal, Sunny, and Christina; all five of us preferring to get as far away as possible before the lights mushroom and explode.

Apparently, we navigate better in the dark when we're running like our lives depend on it. All of us arrive at the chapel within seconds of each other, out of breath and sweating, but intact.

"You were right, Christina, that felt all kind of wrong," Ava says after coming out of the bathroom.

"Yeah, sure. Try a full body pass through, then let me know what you think." Christina takes several gulps from her water bottle while glaring at us. She twists the cap back on and asks, "Why didn't you ignore them?"

"Did you hear what they called me?" Ava mirrors Christina's glare.

"Baby murderer is worse," Christina counters.

"It happened, it's over, so shut up," Gal dismisses all potential for further arguing.

I notice how stressed out Gal is. It bothers me to see him unclench his balled up hands and run trembling fingers through his atypical messy hair. Casually, I stand up from the floor we're all sitting on and shove my hand in one of my pockets like this is a normal thing for me to do after standing.

I say to Gal, "Come over here and look at this old postcard Ava and I found earlier. It has those same women on it we just saw." I pull my hand back out of my pocket and help him up from the floor, putting the valium in the palm of his hand first. Gal expresses the most grateful look I have ever seen on his face.

He dry swallows the pill while we're looking at the postcard. When he points a finger at what I assume is something important he means for me to notice, his finger continues moving along the glass in the shape of a heart. "Is that Ava's ass print?"

My eyes refocus. Sure enough, perfect imprint of ass cheeks on the otherwise crystal clear polished glass. "Mm hmm," I affirm as noncommittally as I can.

Smiling and nodding his approval, Gal leans in and says, "You dirty boy. No wonder you two were gone for so long. Sex in a chapel, I'm gonna have to try that out myself." He glances over his shoulder. "Hmm, think Sunny—"

"Forget it," I interrupt him and look over my shoulder, too. Though Sunny is staring at Ava, as she helps Christina comb the stubborn knots from her hair, he seems a million miles away. "He's in a relationship with someone else. Sounds to me like he's happy. Don't wreck it for him."

"Are you implying I could?"

"Yeah."

"Expound." Gal makes a tsk noise. "Only the flattering parts, please."

"Really? You need your ego stroked now?"

"Actually, I could use something else being stroked right now, but I'll settle for finding out what Payton Raynor *really* thinks about me."

This is more than Gal needing to be flattered; he really does want to know how I view him. It surprises me a little. Though we have never sat down to explicitly discuss the matter, I've always assumed he knew how I felt about him. I don't even need to think about it.

"You would have no problem seducing Sunny, but I know you won't do that because you're a good person. Everybody considers you their best friend, including me. Academically . . . what's there to say? You're valedictorian at graduation, even with a B minus in Spanish. Girls that know you're gay still hit on you, that's how good-looking you are. If I were gay, I'd want to fuck you. I would pay to know how you never get zits. Somehow, you pull off how to be equal parts the voice of reason and the comedic genius. I've seen you on stage many times, you really are a great actor and you'll be an even greater director. The way I treated you earlier tonight should prove to you that one day you'll win an Oscar. I really hope you'll have children one day because I think someone like you should be someone's dad. I think you should have a houseful of kids."

Gal's eyes glisten in the soft glow coming from the chapel's recessed ceiling lights. He clears his throat and says, "Thank you, Payton. That was beautiful and it meant a lot to me." For once, he seems at a loss for words. But this is Gal; he recovers quickly. After wiping dry his eyes, he says, "Yes, I'll marry you."

Chapter Eleven

We've been sitting on the chapel floor for over an hour now. None of us are jumping at the bit to leave the seeming normalcy the closed environment provides. Occasionally, we'll talk, but mostly we've been quiet.

During this time I've made a decision. I'm not taking anyone with me. I will take myself out of this world, and only me. Even my grandfather would say that it is a coward's way to take out others for no good reason, and for once I'll side with him on this one. This is the way I should have been viewing it from the start and I suppose it took a couple of run-ins with ghosts to make me fully realize that.

Truthfully, I think it has more to do with spending time with good friends again. It's helped me realize that there really are decent people out there.

This whole situation has taken on a completely different sort of complexity than what I had imagined. Oddly enough, I'm finding myself half-wanting to figure out a way to get them out of Silentis and spend my last night alone with entities I assume I'll join once I put a bullet in my head. To be honest, though, those things out there scare the hell out of me.

Sunny is the one who's been the quietest since we got here, but finally he speaks up.

"I've been thinking about it," he says to no one in particular. "It seems like these ghosts we're seeing do their own thing. They're oblivious to what's really going on around them unless someone inserts a current event, or memory, or a thought. There may be something to them having to pass through a living person at the same time, too. I don't know." He looks at us and shrugs. "We would have to test it to know for sure."

The hint lingers in the air like the stench left over after someone takes a shit.

"Are you crazy?" Gal asks him what we're all thinking.

"Possibly, but I'm willing to try it myself. Well, that is if you guys will stand watch and help me out if I pick a shithead ghost who doesn't explode."

All of us are too intrigued at this point to entertain the idea of trying to talk Sunny out of it. This intrigue comes in the form of complete silence, lots of eye-blinking, and—for me at least—considering the possibilities since the idea has merit.

He almost seems disappointed when Ava asks, "How'd you want to go about it?"

Sunny kind of grimaces at us before explaining, "Mrs. White was really aggressive, but I think that was because she was dealing with a baby she knew was sick and probably gonna die. Those Smith daughters weren't like that since their father was already dead. Either way, they disappear, explode, whatever, when their role-playing gets interrupted. To prove it, I'll interrupt one on purpose and then we'll see what happens."

"What do we do if it doesn't explode?" Christina asks.

"Run," Sunny offers his best guess. "Like we've been doing when one does explode. Hopefully, one of you will make sure I'm running, too."

* * *

It feels like we've been walking around for more than an hour and so far, we haven't seen or heard anything, save the biggest raccoon I have ever encountered.

We're standing in a dark shadow cast by the tallest obelisk in Silentis, haggling over which area to try next, when a female's screaming brings our debate to a dead stop. Even coonzilla pauses before running off toward the creek.

All of us spin around to the source and find two entities; a man and the woman he's choking, but not so forcefully as to kill her. When she finally slumps to the ground, the man looks over his shoulder and his lips curl into a cruel smile.

They're adults, but they seem small. Like how things appear smaller from a distance, yet we are standing close enough that they shouldn't look this way.

Sunny tries repeatedly to interrupt them when the memory replays itself. He even punches the man—his fist only goes through the dark form—and yells at him to leave the woman alone. The shimmering dark entities sputter out and a few minutes after Sunny comes back to stand beside us, a scream splits the air again.

"I guess my theory was wrong," Sunny says.

The only one still watching the scene unfold again is Gal. His brow is furrowed, like he's trying to solve a trigonometry test question.

"Something is different this time," Gal whispers. "It's like we're watching someone's memory of that event, like when we heard a knock on the door with Mrs. White. That might explain why those two look so small."

"You're smart for a queer," says a man's deep voice from behind us. "You're also standing in the way. I *was* teaching my son how to deal with his wife's insolent behavior."

We whirl toward the voice. This one is so much darker than the others, almost impossible to see, forcing us to give him our full attention. Since he's more interested in us now, the two in the memory have vanished. There is nothing but eerie silence while the entity stares menacingly at Gal.

"Not that you would understand anything about women."

Something sinister evolves in Gal's expression. "I know you're not supposed to abuse them," he spat. "How 'bout you get your nasty ass back to hell."

Gal shoves both his hands through the center of the ghost's chest. We underestimate this aberration's capacity for evil. It chuckles and, to our new horror, grabs Gal's wrists. "Won't you come with me, sweetheart?"

Without hesitation or need to discuss the matter first, the rest of us plow through the entity—literally *through* it. I reach for Christina before she falls and Sunny and Ava slam into each other. With the hideous chuckling morphing into sadistic laughter, the point of light finally forms. Thankfully, in its face, silencing the son of a bitch.

All of us take instant notice of the violent potential this explosion is going to have. The light itself seems agitated by the ghost's reluctance to let go, whose hands are snatching blindly in the air to reclaim Gal's wrists.

"Run!"

I don't know who screams this, it could have been me. I don't even know if the voice is male or female. But it's perfectly sound advice and that is exactly what we all do.

This time we manage to run as a group, so we end up together on the back side of the Vanderhorst Mausoleum. I think we're all hoping the same thing: that we didn't run from insanity and straight into chaos.

While catching his breath and looking at where we ended up, Gal says, "Oh, God, please, let all my ancestors be at peace. Or at least not evil assholes."

"You okay?" I ask him. He nods and sighs his relief that he really is okay. I put my hand on his shoulder and give him a reassuring pat. "You don't have anything to worry about, the Vanderhorst family is a good one. Well, until the lawyers came along." Gal gives me an eat shit look, which makes me laugh. "I'm just kidding you. Sounds to me like your parents are working on some great causes. Speaking of which, you got any watermelon candy left?"

We step inside the Vanderhorst Mausoleum and no matter what I've said about the family, we're all still jumpy from our last experience. God forbid one of us steps on a bit of gravel or a twig. I almost wish I'd have brought the higher milligram valium. Unfortunately, we would all pass out and who knows what kind of pranks ghosts pull on sleeping teenagers.

"Why was Mr. Shealy able to stick around so long?" Gal asks anyone. "And why was he able to hold on to me?"

"What makes you think it was Mr. Shealy?" Sunny asks.

"I just assumed it was." Gal shrugs. "We were by the Shealy family obelisk. It's one of the ones I took notes on earlier."

Sunny paces back and forth a few times and stops in front of an older Vanderhorst wall plaque, but doesn't say anything.

"What if we're one of them?" Christina mumbles, more to herself, but we all hear the question.

Ava walks over to her. "What do you mean?"

Christina shakes her head. A look of agony washes over her face at having to say it. "What if we all died somewhere along the way? What if we're seeing these things because we are one now?"

"That's not possible," I say.

Her head snaps to me. She looks at me through narrowed eyes. There seems an accusation in her expression and a bit of anger laced with what almost looks like a tinge of hatred. "Really?" Christina blurts out. "How are you so sure of that?"

It's kind of a surreal moment for me, given what I had been planning before. I even traipse through my memories to make sure I hadn't really shot us all. There is a lot to account for, but short of pulling the gun and mags out of my backpack to count bullets, I'm rather positive I haven't killed anyone tonight.

Aside from Sunny, who's still staring at the wall in deep thought, everyone else is looking at me. I have to give something for an answer.

"Well," I begin, trying to come up with something plausible on the spot, "wouldn't we be haunting wherever our bodies lay?"

The accusatory look, the one I hope I'm misinterpreting, gives way to the consideration that I may have a point. Christina's eyes dart along the mausoleum's floor, looking for our dead bodies, I suppose.

Maybe it's one of those monkey-see, monkey-do things, but when Gal and Ava start glancing at the dark corners, so do I. The only dead things in here are vaulted Vanderhorsts and legs-up cockroaches.

Rather than admit that I have a point, she shrugs and says, "Yeah, well . . ." and leaves it open-ended in case another idea comes to her later.

"We're not dead." Sunny turns around and gives us a thorough visual exam. "You all look solid to me and even Mr. Shealy said he couldn't see through Gal. I think we can safely assume we're still amongst the living."

"I certainly hope so." Gal's relief is so blatantly obvious—portrayed on his face by restored confidence, as though he had been stressing out about it since the possibility had left Christina's lips. "There's a whole ton of shit I still want to do."

"I wonder if paying attention to them during the day makes it more likely that they'll reenact memories at night." Sunny goes over to the mausoleum opening and peers out into the dark. "We never went to the newer section of Silentis since it was closed off for lawn maintenance. You guys want to check it out and see if anything is going on over there?"

"I'd rather go back to the front gate and wait for someone to drive by so we can get out of here," Gal says and Ava nods in agreement.

"Come on. It won't take us long," Sunny urges.

"I'm curious, too, actually." Christina joins Sunny by the door and waits for the rest of us to get on the crazy train. "We're already close to the newer part of the cemetery anyway. And we have all night to wait around by the front gate for *no one*."

"Fine." Gal sighs loudly for everyone's benefit. "But only if we all stick close together." He stomps over toward the open doorway, warning us all on the way as though we have any say in the matter, "I better not regret this."

Ava looks at me, wearing a huge question mark in her expression.

"Up for some more scary shit that we'll probably have to run from?" I ask rather than answer her unspoken question.

"Not really, but I don't have any other plans at the moment," she says, sounding tired and reluctant. Now I'm wishing I would have said what she wanted to hear.

"Hey, you don't have to do this just because they want to. I'll walk back with you to the front gate if you're done seeing these weird things," I tell her and offer my best understanding smile. "I know *I* wouldn't mind not seeing them anymore." I'm trying to provide her with an easy out in case she really is that scared and doesn't want to admit it.

The war between her conflicting ideals is so apparent in her eyes. I know she's on to my attempt to be chivalrous when she narrows her eyes at me just slightly. "Gal's right, we need to stay in a group. And I'd be lying if I said I wasn't a little curious myself." Ava holds her hand out to me and cracks a smile. "You can hold my hand, I'll protect you. Unless you want to hold Gal's."

"That's okay." I take her hand. "I don't like the ghosts he hangs out with."

"Homophobe," Gal says without turning around to look at me.

"Fairy," I shoot back.

We leave the Vanderhorst Mausoleum, and intentionally skirt the edge of Silentis, walking along the path abutting the marsh to get to the newer section.

Any time we hear something that's not the wind or from some nocturnal animal, it goes unmentioned, unexplored, and unwitnessed. We keep our eyes trained forward until we're out of range and then one of us will broach a neutral subject.

While trying to ignore what sounds like a mournful husband crying over the loss of his wife and newborn son, Gal brings up the sticky parent subject to squash all notion anyone may have of detouring from our arrangement.

"So, which one of you won't be attending prom because your parents won't let you out of the house after not coming home tonight?"

"My parents won't worry," Christina says. "They're opening a new pharmacy on the east side. They haven't been getting home till late for the past month. They'll just think I've already gone to bed."

"Mine are working late, too," Gal says. "They may not even notice my car isn't parked by the road till morning. Even then, they'll probably just assume I left for school early."

"Thankfully, mine are in London on their twentieth wedding anniversary," Sunny adds to the list of parents who won't notice their kids are missing. "They're flying back tomorrow."

"I don't know," I sort of say and mumble at the same time.

With my mom, it depends on whether or not she's going through a bad spell, which she has been lately. My dad has been clingy since Wade died, but less so this past month because he's busy with maintenance flights at Charleston Airforce Base.

Then I remember, it doesn't matter because I'm not going back home.

"It's hard to say with my parents," I add when it feels like too many quiet seconds have ticked by.

A no-brainer really, Ava (Gal, too) knows a good bit about my fucked up family dynamics, so she steers the conversation to her own parents.

"My dad never needs much of a reason to ground me. But he's a softie, he'll cave after two days. I have no doubt my mom has already blown up my cellphone with calls and texts. I'm sure the back of Gal's car is ready to kick my phone out into the parking lot. My mom is weird. She can be really cool about some things, but then she's also controlling."

Dammit, why did she have to mention Mrs. Caddo? Instantly, my entire body flinches and I guess Ava must have felt it through our still joined hands because I can feel her staring up at me while we continue walking. I sneak a glance at her and see the questioning frown on her face.

"I want to talk to you about something," I say and nod toward the other three walking ahead of us. "Preferably alone, if we get the chance."

"Okay, we'll see how it goes," is all she says of the likelihood of us being able to speak privately.

There is a certain clarity in her tone, and on her face. I've never been completely sure if Ava has her own suspicions about her mother and my father. I had kind of hoped she was still innocent to it, but now I'm pretty sure she already knows. I can almost feel this unspoken knowledge between us.

* * *

It takes longer to get there than we thought it would. No doubt due to our refusal to take the shortcuts through the cemetery. But we're here and have been for a while, watching and seeing nothing at all occur. Sunny, Gal, and Christina come up with a plan to start researching headstones and see if anything comes of it.

Ava and I stare at them blankly as they walk over to the nearby graves, leaving us with that private moment I hadn't *really* expected to get.

I'm not sure what to do and I'm already trying to come up with a way to artfully dodge my own request to talk to her as we sit down on a granite wall surrounding the Seabrook family.

As though angels came down and whispered into her ear, Ava ends my torture and asks, "Does what you want to talk to me about have anything to do with our parents?"

"Yeah," I answer like a chicken-shit.

"Two in particular?"

"Yeah." I can't believe how much of a coward I'm being by letting her do all the talking in this messed up conversation.

I hear a smidge of an emotional edge in her voice when she braves, "How long have you known?"

"Since the beginning of last year." I focus my eyes on the nearest tree trunk and imagine what creatures must live in the numerous cavities in the effort to block out the image of my father and Ava's mother. "What about you?" I hear myself ask.

"About that same time." Ava takes an audible breath. "I think my father suspects it. He doesn't know who she's having an affair with, but he knows something is going on."

Finally, I look at her and I can see how worried she is. She shivers even though it's a million degrees. Her eyes reflect a little too much of what little light we have.

She won't cry, though. Not over this, and not in public. But I know her well enough to know she would cry if she weren't so stubborn. I don't know if it is for my sake, her own, or for both our families, but I really hate what it's doing to us.

"They're being selfish jerks and it pisses me off that it's messing with our lives," I tell her and hope she gets what I wish I could say, but won't since I'm still too afraid to. And because, just like her, I'm too stubborn.

"You've summed it up exactly." She leans in with a full-body nudge. "They're selfish jerks. Let's not talk about them anymore."

"Works for me." I hop down from the wall and help her down. Once we catch up to the others, I ask them, "Have you seen anything?"

"Nothing, not even a whisper," Sunny says. "Kind of interesting, huh?"

"I guess." Nothing about this night seems rational to me. "There has to be an explanation for what's going on. I mentioned to Ava earlier that we could be having hallucinations from all the crap we've been ingesting."

Sunny snorts at the notion. "We're all having the same hallucinations? At the same time? Come on, Payton. Really?"

"Oh? So, a haunted cemetery makes more sense than the drug-induced hallucinations of teenagers' theory?"

"Were the original architect and caretakers on pot and valium?"

"Put your dicks away and come look at this," Gal calls over to me and Sunny.

Christina, Ava, and Gal are standing in front of the Herndon marble archway memorial. Sunny and I give each other a half-hearted sneer and join them to see what they find so fascinating.

The entire opening has a shimmering quality to it, much like the entities we've been seeing, but with more exactness. I walk around to the other side and it looks the same way, and I can see the others through the shimmering wall.

"Can you see me?" I ask them. They all nod and I come back around to the front.

"What do you think it is?" Christina asks.

"Not a clue." I inch my hand toward the open archway, but Ava slaps it away before I make contact.

"Don't touch it!" Her eyes are wide open, somewhat fearful. "Look. Someone's there."

Four heads turn from Ava to the archway and sure enough, we see another person there. She's looking right back at us, too, and seems just as confused by our presence as we are of hers. Her hair is arranged in what must be hundreds of blonde—almost white—tiny slivers of braids. She clutches a bed sheet closer to her chest and looks to her right at someone approaching her.

When he comes into our view, he's not wearing a bed sheet . . . or anything else. Neither one of them look much older than we are, at least his ass doesn't.

"Well, well," Gal says, "finally something not scary."

The ass spins around at the sound of Gal's vocalized appreciation and sees us staring at him—now his nude front. Thankfully, he grabs a corner of the girl's sheet and asks her who we are.

"I don't know," she answers him. As she leans forward and reaches for some object out of range of the archway view, she adds, "This is the first time I've seen anyone there. Normally—"

They vanish, along with the rest of the girl's answer, and the archway goes back to being just that— an oversized marble memorial for families rich enough to afford it.

"That was different," Christina says and sticks her arm through the archway.

"It was," Sunny agrees. He sighs and turns to me. "Perhaps you're right, Payton. That girl wasn't expecting anyone to be here. It makes me think there *could* be a rational explanation for what we've been seeing. I'm just not convinced it's hallucinations."

"Maybe we're all on a TV show." Gal squints at all the trees nearest the lamp posts and shines a flashlight on a mausoleum opening. "Like one of those hidden camera shows."

Though it would explain a lot, that's the last thing I want it to be. There would have to be camera crews somewhere nearby and this would ruin my plans. "Let's head back to the front gate." I take off without waiting to hear if they have any problems with it.

Chapter Twelve

To call the area we're leaving behind the 'newer' section of Silentis is misleading. Sure, it's *new*, if you consider a hundred years ago to be recent times.

That was when the board acquired the land from the defunct golf course of a prestigious country club. It went out of business when the river decided to sink the first three fairways. I feel certain the antiquated men's only status had also reached the end of its glory days.

When the country club reopened on the other side of the river, gender was no longer a qualifier for membership, just shitloads of money.

"Hey, let's fill up our water bottles now." Gal stoops by a spigot, but keeps a watchful eye on the oldest section of Silentis. We will have to walk through it to get to the front gate. "I'd rather not be dehydrated while we tiptoe through crazy town." He shines his flashlight through the refilled water bottle and sighs. "Why did I look?"

We take our time filling water bottles. Wasting time to be honest, prolonging the moment we'll have to march past the multitudes of graves we researched throughout the day. Briefly, we discuss walking back to the entrance by following alongside the cemetery's walls.

"Nah, it'll just take longer," Sunny says. "Plus, I remember that's where a lot of war memorials are and I really don't want to be a part of someone's battle memory."

I'm guessing we have taken roughly ten brisk steps in—okay, maybe twenty, tops . . . definitely no more than thirty to fifty fast-paced steps—and we see the small figure of a little girl picking unseen berries at the edge of a family plot.

With every five or so, she selects one to consume right away and puts the rest in a tin bucket by her bare feet. It seems like a neutral enough reenactment, but we don't stick around long to find out otherwise.

Several plots along and we see a wedding ceremony that prompts Ava to urge the rest of us to move faster.

Once we reach the next lamp post, Ava stops us. "That groom and bride back there? They died in a church fire. *On* their wedding day. It's on their tombstone that they were buried together in his family plot since they had completed their vows before the Great Charleston fire of 1861."

What can I say? It's a natural reaction. We all glance in the direction of the newlyweds, half-expecting to see chaos in flames, but rather we find the little berry-picking girl had followed us.

"I think I'm lost," she says. "Can you help me?"

For some reason, everyone looks at me, including the little girl. Then it occurs to me who she might be. I'm pretty sure I was standing near her grave while I eavesdropped on Gal and Ava's conversation earlier.

"Is your name Minnie Nattalie?" I ask her.

"Yes, sir."

Wow, I don't think I've ever been called *sir* before. I'm right about who she is. Hers was the one headstone I read twice, because it had no date of birth or death and it had a carving of a little girl kneeling at her bedside in prayer. Other than her name, the only inscription was, 'A mother's only child.'

Looking at Minnie's spectral memory self, that which is smiling up at me in my reality, I'm happy to meet her. However, I also feel like it's my responsibility to send her back to the bedside prayer, that which is Minnie's reality.

"I'll help you. Will you take my hand?"

Minnie nods and reaches for my hand. Her light is tiny and instant. It builds and mushrooms in a delicate way. If all the entities were as soft and pliant, it wouldn't be so bad. When she's gone, some part of me wishes she was still here.

"That was sweet, Payton," Christina says. "Let's keep moving, okay? We still have a ways to go."

* * *

We pass by a general refusing to surrender, the entire H. L. Hunley submarine crew making their peace with God before they drown, several more parents weeping for their dead children, and (oddly enough) a hunting dog returning to some unseen hunter with a limp mallard clutched firmly in its jaws.

Each time a reenacting memory materializes, all five of us look up for the visual, but otherwise we remain quiet and uninvolved and continue trudging forward. Gal's at the front of the silent line and veers off toward the chapel when we near it.

Though a ghost-free environment, no one speaks while we wait for our turn to use the chapel bathroom. I go last. While I'm in here I check the time on my cellphone. I haven't been able to for a while because it would stand out like a cheap Christmas tree in the dark. I'm shocked—it's almost midnight. I hate that it's that late already.

There's a voice message from my dad and though curious, I'm not about to listen to it. I don't trust my ability to listen to a family member's voice right now. I'd crumble for sure. Particularly, my dad's. His voice reminds me too much of Wade's.

Unzipping the longest zipper in the history of backpacks, I hesitate a moment before I ready the gun for later.

Do I want to do this? I think about what my life has been like up to this moment. I'm happy tonight has been a reprieve from all the usual bullshit. Even with all the unexpected, inexplicable, maybe-it-is-hallucinations moments of this supremely insane night, I'm glad to have had the opportunity to spend it with Gal and Ava. And, yes, even Sunny and Christina.

But I still want to do this. There is no future for me. Not the one I want to have. I'm stuck in a misery I don't know any other way out of. I can't even stand the thought that we will have to pass right by the Raynor Mausoleum on our way to the front gate, but I'll take averse comfort in knowing it will be my new home soon. After inserting the mag and making sure the safety feature is on, I tuck it away again.

When I come back out of the bathroom, the others are already engaged in conversation.

"Have you guys noticed that some of them aren't as hard to see as others?" I hear Christina asking.

"Yeah, I noticed that, too. Maybe they get stronger the later it gets," Sunny says.

"I still want to know what was up with those two we saw in the archway." Ava frowns at Gal. "You really think it's all a hoax?"

"No," he answers. "That girl was surprised to see us. Neither one of them looked like what we've been seeing tonight. I have this feeling that she was wanting to show him something, and it wasn't us. I think that's why she shut it down so quickly."

"It could be they were doing some kind of a paranormal investigation," Sunny suggests.

"Wouldn't they have called the cops by now?" I ask.

"Not if they didn't have approval," Gal says.

I'm thinking about *how* we saw them. "Gal, have you ever seen that kind of technology before?"

"Nope." Gal laughs and snorts simultaneously. "But then again, I'm not planning on being a film director for ghost hunters. I have no idea what sort of equipment they use."

"I wonder if they would show up in a photo . . ." Sunny lets the statement dangle in the air, but he's eyeing me in particular. "What do you think, Payton?"

"I think I just got drafted."

Actually, I don't really mind going out there again. I'm starting to feel caged. The air in here is stagnant, like it needs and wants a fresh breeze as much I do.

Solution? One strawberry and one banana flavored pot candy together ought to fix that. I toss the wrappers in my bag and pull out my camera. After I make a few adjustments to the settings for recording in the dark, I go over to the door where Gal is waiting.

"You don't have to come with me," I tell him.

I get one raised eyebrow and then an eye roll. He says, "I'm not letting you go out there alone. I'd appreciate it if we didn't do the ten minute back and forth arguing routine before I end up going with you anyway."

"Fine." I smile, just a smidge. "Are we holding hands?"

"Don't make me kick your ass," he says and opens the door.

* * *

Gal and I leave the chapel and we're both stumped by the lack of activity. Either ghosts quit at midnight or they're all on break. We decide to wait it out rather than venture too far from the chapel.

I nudge Gal when I spot the dark figure of a woman standing in front of the Legare Mausoleum entrance. All I need is to move in close enough to get decent video footage, so we creep along one headstone at a time. When I'm as close as I care for us to be, I position her in the view finder and press record.

"Hey, I was just kidding back there at the chapel. We can hold hands if you want," Gal whispers to me after a few (way too long) minutes of mutual staring between us and the female entity. "Is it just my imagination, or is she watching us?"

I lower my camera and study her with my own eyes. It does seem like she is focusing her attention directly at us, but it's hard to know for sure at this distance. I tug at Gal's elbow and get him to follow me over to a different location a few yards away. When we stop, she's still facing us.

"Let's go back to the chapel," I whisper. "I filmed enough to be able to answer our question."

We haven't moved yet and she says, "Don't go. I want to speak to you, please."

"Is she talking to us?" Gal asks me.

A quick survey of our surroundings doesn't reveal any other entities so I assume she must be. "I think so. What do you want to do?"

"Well, she *is* being polite. She said please." Gal gives me a sort of reluctant grimace of surrender. "I'd hate to find out that ignoring her will come at a price. Know what I mean?"

"Yeah, I know." I consider where she's at. "Well, obviously, she's a Legare. Maybe she'll be nice to us since you're related to her."

"No pressure, huh?"

"Are we gonna see what she wants or not?"

"I'm still deciding, Payton, stop rushing me."

"Boys, I can hear you," the woman says. "I have no intentions of scaring either one of you. I only want to give a message to Payton and then I hope Gal will be so kind as to send me back."

We're dumbstruck and frozen in place, not unlike the angel statues surrounding us. "Um," is all Gal says.

"Message," is all I mumble. I assume we look and sound like idiots.

"Please, come closer," she says. "Those of us in mausoleums are somewhat restricted with where we can go. I cannot wander about as some do here."

There is a smooth, coaxing gentleness in her voice. It hints at the possibility that she very well could be like one of the calmer entities we've encountered tonight.

We don't discuss it. Instead, we obey and shuffle over to her, side by side, and so close to each other that we may as well be holding hands. However, we do stop a few feet in front of her; a proper head-start run distance away just in case it turns out she's not so nice after all.

The Legare lady isn't as dark up close, a bit like some of the other entities we have been noticing recently. Particularly, her facial features are more defined and she's actually quite stunning. So much so that I almost want to ask Gal what he thinks, but since she's smiling and aware of our presence, I guess that would be considered rude.

Though still scared and fueled by adrenaline, I gawk silently as an alternative, like most teenage boys do. (That would be the other hormone fueling my daily existence.)

"You want me to touch you?" I can't believe Gal asks her.

Her smile broadens and I'm sure she would laugh under normal circumstances. "I do," she answers him, "but first I need to say something to Payton."

That's right, I'd forgotten all about this message she wanted to give me. For a fleeting second, I worry she may know of my plans. I force myself to relax by realizing someone from the past couldn't possibly know about someone else's future. Still, it is unnerving as I can't fathom what else it could be.

"Your brother wants to see you."

This simple statement scares me more than anything else has this entire night.

"What?" I'm fighting the urge to look over in the direction of the Raynor Mausoleum.

"Wade wants to talk to you," she says. "He knows you're here."

A rush of panic threatens to send me running back to the chapel, but the hope that she will pass a message back to Wade keeps me grounded. "I can't."

"You don't have to. Like me, he cannot leave his family tomb. You will have to go to Wade if you choose to see him."

"Do you know why he wants to see me?"

"No." She edges closer to me, just slightly. I assume it's as far as she can go. "All I know is that it's important to him that he has the chance to talk to you."

"I have to think about it."

"I understand. You have until dawn to decide." She turns to Gal and there seems a fondness in her eyes. "You can touch me now."

Gal is still gawking in disbelief and doesn't snap out of it until I nudge him. "Okay, wait. Can I ask you something first?"

"Of course."

"Is all of this really happening?" Gal blinks a few times and shakes his head. "I mean . . . are you a ghost? Is that what we've been seeing?"

"Yes, but you knew that already." She appears lost in her own thoughts for a moment. "Silentis is a very unique place."

Just before Gal reaches for her, I blurt out my own request for knowledge. "We saw two people earlier and they didn't look like what we've been seeing. They looked more like us." I feel insensitive for the 'us' reference and I truly hope she doesn't have issues with being dead. "Do you know anything about them?"

"I'm not sure. Perhaps they were from the seat of Silentis." Something shifts in the totality of whatever it is that comprises her reason for being here. There's a second when she looks at me, staring hard at whatever comprises *my* totality, and I observe a hint of budding hatred forming in her expression before she says to Gal, "Do it now . . . quickly."

His brow creases. He must be as confused by her abruptness as I am. But he does as she requests. It's the fastest exit we have seen yet. Maybe she remembered that Legares don't like Raynors.

Chapter Thirteen

"That was sudden," Gal says when she's gone.

"Yeah."

I'm just grateful that he doesn't blame me for her hasty departure. Or, if he does, then for the fact that he's hiding it from me at least. While leading him away from the Legare Mausoleum entrance, I ask, "What do you think the seat of Silentis means?"

"I don't have a clue, but I'm not gonna let you get away with avoiding a certain subject." Gal grabs my arm to keep me from retreating. "Assuming all this crazy shit is really happening to us, what are you planning to do about Wade?"

Hearing my brother's name spoken aloud is a tormenting hell for me and I have been forced to hear it several times tonight. When his name rolls off my own tongue, it's also a special kind of hell, one that actually causes me physical pain.

"So, you're still having doubts about what's going on here?" This is all I can get out of my mouth.

"Payton."

"Dammit, Gal, you know how hard it is for me!"

"I do know that." His beautifully compassionate voice seeks to soothe me. "It's just you and me, okay? Tell me how you want to handle this."

"I can't go in there alone, Gal." My God, I feel like I want to cry. "It still hurts me too much. I just can't."

It's a delicate thing between two men, made even more so when one of them is gay, but Gal ignores it and pulls me into a hug.

My need for comfort is so overwhelming that I don't care how I must seem to him, myself, or to the rest of the whole wide world. I cling to him as though the world would stop spinning for everyone if I didn't allow myself this thankful moment to fall to pieces. Interestingly, though I go through the motions, I manage to suppress the teary part of my breakdown.

A sense of something normal returns to me—a rippling calm that flows from Gal to me, then back to Gal. With the calm comes the awkwardness, and it parts us. I say, "Sorry, bro. I didn't mean to . . . you know, burden you and stuff."

Famous eye roll, of course. "You're so heterosexual, you know that?"

"You say that like it's a bad thing."

"It's not anything but a fact, Payton." He frogs my arm, probably for the sole purpose of solidifying my need to substantiate our bro-ness. His expression turns to that parental caring that I love so much about him. "You don't have to go in there at all if you don't want to. But if you do, you're not alone. Okay?"

"Thank you." I nod like I'm in the midst of convincing myself. "I still need time to think about it."

"Come on, let's get back to the chapel before they file a missing person's report on us."

* * *

We get back and all of us pile up in front of my laptop. Though Gal and I had seen the entity first hand, we're still excited to find out whether or not she will show up on video.

I half-expect to see nothing, but to my surprise we discover a slight disturbance in the area where the woman was standing. It's not as clear as in person, but you can see that something else is there.

The disappointment comes when the only part of the conversation that is audible are the times when Gal and I were speaking. When the woman speaks, it sounds more like wind, or the way a seashell sounds when you hold it up to your ear and if someone were whispering to you from the other side of it.

"Who wants to see you?" Ava asks me. A lump forms in my throat and it hurts like hell. I can't answer her and she guesses, "Wade?"

"Yeah," I answer in a trembling breath while staring at the floor.

"Your dead brother wants to see you?" Christina asks, rather loud about it too, like she's shocked.

I'm beginning to understand why people think she's a freak. It's getting harder not to call her that myself.

"Apparently so." I can hear the cold edge in my voice and I try not to think about how it reminds me of the way my grandfather sounds when someone pushes his evil button. "That was the message anyway."

What a piece of work she is. Not even a flinch before she says, "I think you should find out what he wants. You could regret it later if you didn't."

"Christina, that's enough," Ava says and takes my hand. "Will you come with me to the front of the chapel? I want to talk to you privately."

We sit down on the front pew and the first thing she wants to know is, "Are you all right?"

"About potentially seeing Wade?"

"You don't have to, you know."

"That's what the Legare woman said."

"Maybe you shouldn't."

"Why do you say that?"

"Because I know you blame yourself for Wade's death."

Her statement causes an instant wrinkle on my forehead. "How could you possibly know that?"

"I'm not stupid, Payton." She glowers at me, but it's more of a chastising sort of expression. "I grew up with you and I know how you are with some things. I also know how close you and Wade were. All I'm saying is that if you think seeing him again will be too painful, then don't do it."

"He was on the phone with me when he ran off the road."

Ava gives my hand a firm squeeze and says, "It's still not your fault. You guys talked all the time on the phone after he went to the Citadel. Wade travelled that road every weekend . . . even while on the phone with you. I remember it well because you would ignore me and I would get jealous. There are other possibilities for why he veered off the road and hit that tree."

"I miss him so much, Ava," I say, and then I cry.

Weird, isn't it? I can cry in front of a girl, but not a guy. I don't know what crazy logic this is. Maybe it's because guys perceive females as soft and gentle, and understanding beings.

Not so strange is how I'll take the bro-hug from Gal, but only allow Ava to lean against my shoulder while I wipe my eyes dry.

This, however, is not a mystery. A frontal hug from Ava would probably produce a hard-on that does not pair well with the moment. Hell, just having thought about it caused some stiffening.

"Sorry for the wet emotions," I say after a sniff.

"Shut up." She sighs and asks, "Did the Legare woman say what Wade wanted to talk to you about?"

"No."

"You gonna do it?"

"I'm still thinking about it."

"Well, you're not doing it alone."

"That's what Gal said." We both laugh.

Ava gets up and walks over to the pulpit, searching for something by the way she's peering into every nook and cranny. "You planning to give me a sermon?"

"You'd think there would be a box of tissues in a cemetery chapel, right?" She disappears on the other side of the platform and all I see and hear are the pulpit's cabinet doors opening and closing. "Holy shit!"

"What?"

She stands up, mischief glinting in her eyes and wide smile, holding a bottle in her right hand. "Not one single tissue, but an almost full bottle of drown your sorrows bourbon hidden behind an empty donations box."

"Did I hear someone say bourbon?" Gal appears like magic.

I hear music playing. My music. From my laptop. "You opened my music library?"

"Yeah."

"Prick."

"That's Mr. DJ Prick, thank you very much." He flops down on the pew where Ava had been sitting. Christina and Sunny take a pew on the other side of the center aisle. "It just started raining outside," Gal informs me and Ava. "I say we sample that bourbon and dance on the pews to Payton's song list."

Several passes of the bourbon bottle loosens everyone up. It takes me the longest to join the dance group and I'm sure it has a lot to do with watching Gal dance with Ava. I never knew I had a jealous streak in me and I can't believe how awful it feels.

It's only when I cut in and shoo Gal away that this hideous green monster leaves me alone.

Unfortunately, one hell replaces another and it's not long before I'm dancing her closer toward the bathroom.

Earlier, on that table with the old postcards, she was like an unexpected gift for me. Like the kind your parents hide on Christmas morning and only give to you after you've ripped open every present under the tree and have begrudgingly accepted that what you really wanted isn't among the loot and litter.

When she was beneath me by the gatekeeper's building, it was like what I imagine heaven would be if it were tailored specifically for me. As she shudders and moans above me on the chapel bathroom floor with music playing on the other side of the shut door, and with my hands splayed out on her backside to pull her against me as close as possible before the beautiful colors explode inside my head . . . Ava. Is. My. God. I worship no other.

* * *

Ava and I exit the bathroom to find Sunny standing in front of the pulpit feeding a wafer each to Gal and Christina. They're kneeling before him and trying to keep their snickering at a minimum.

"What are you doing?" I ask them.

"Holy Communion," Sunny answers.

"Where did you find those wafers?" Ava's eyes widen and she rushes over to snatch a few for herself.

"In the bench behind the pulpit." Sunny goes over to it and pulls out several more boxes of them. "They're probably kept on hand for the Catholics."

Five teenagers with: bellies full of Catholic crackers and Baptist bourbon, cushioned pews, and the sound of pattering rain in the middle of the night—you have the perfect ambiance for a quick nap. When I beg (nag, really) Ava to share a pew with me, and after she tells me there is no way we could both fit on one together, she relents to sleep on the top altar stair with me.

I don't want to leave this world not knowing what it's like to spoon with someone. I have to say, it feels fantastic.

Chapter Fourteen

A monotonous swishing sound wakes me up. I'm confused by the unfamiliar surroundings for a second, but then I see (and taste) Ava's hair as it's fanned out in every direction and I remember where I'm at.

Sitting up, I see Gal is already awake and frantically trying to tell me with gestures only to be quiet. He points to the area by the chapel's front doors and I see an entity busying himself with sweeping the floor.

"Oh, Fada, puhtek me fom dese yuh schemy buckruh plateyes," he mumbles the Gullah words, but it's loud enough to wake up everyone else. Christina gasps when she sees him and he stops sweeping to stare directly at each of us. "Don' gimme no truble now, haints. Jis' lemme gitt'ru wu'kn yuh."

He doesn't go back to sweeping, though, just continues to stare at us. We each receive several generous seconds of wide-eyed scrutiny before he moves on to the next. It becomes more and more obvious that it's a stand-off on who is going to move first.

Sunny slides off the pew and goes to him. He's about to touch him, but pauses when the old guy says, "Don' boddun yasef, suh, A gwine't mek de chu'ch flo' shine."

"You don't have to do that anymore," Sunny says and puts his hand through the man's center.

Rather than a light building to explosion, this entity leaves by way of popping out like a soap bubble.

"How could we have been so evil?" Gal questions the grotesque history.

"*Been*?" I half-laugh, half-snort, thinking of the abysmal reality of ongoing oppression. "I assure you, Gal, all of you . . ." My gaze flicks to Ava, then to Sunny, and finally Christina, "We're not done."

He may have been pushing a broom from 1850, but the *indulgent* and *generous* Masters are still out there, still dirtying up the floor, and still insisting someone else clean the mess for as close to free as possible. But, hey . . . at least now they provide the cheap-ass brooms to get the job done.

"It stopped raining," Sunny says from the chapel doorway. "Let's go back to the front gate and wait there."

* * *

While everyone mills around by the bathroom door, waiting for their turn, I discreetly set my camera down on the farthest end of the first pew. It goes against my nature to leave it like this, but for that very reason it's also my insurance policy. Having to retrieve it because it's a precious thing to me will give me the opportunity to be alone later.

A quick check of the time reveals it's almost 2:00 a.m. That's not a lot of hours left for me. I still haven't made up my mind about going to the Raynor Mausoleum. Every time I give it consideration, my stomach churns from the stress and I have to shift my focus to something else.

"I'd kill for a toothbrush right now," Ava says when she walks out of the bathroom and I wish I had a magic wand to conjure one up for her.

"I don't have a toothbrush, but if it'll keep you from murdering anyone I have a mint," Gal says and offers her a mint flavored pot candy.

"I like mint, too, asshole," I mimic his earlier comment about the valium.

He hands me one, and one each to Christina's and Sunny's outstretched waiting hands. "That's it. I don't have any more mint ones left, you greedy bastards."

We step out of the chapel and into the sauna-like atmosphere of a southern cemetery after a late spring rain. Sweat beads form on everyone's face within seconds and mosquitoes swarm around every inch of exposed skin, forcing us back inside to reapply Gal's bug repellent.

After dousing myself, finishing last at my ankles, I hold the half-empty bottle up to Gal and smile at him. "You thinking to bring this is a perfect example of why I think you're the smartest person I know."

"I know." He sighs with dramatic flair. "Being a genius has its perks." He offers me his hand to help me up. "You may rise now, adoring fan."

Though the mosquitoes back off, the balmy environment maintains its unrelenting grip on us. Our towels, now draped around our necks, have become the sweat absorbing must-have for perspiring teenagers.

"I long for air-conditioning," Christina voices all our thoughts. "Hold on, guys."

She stops and takes off her backpack, propping it on top of the nearest headstone. After a minute or so of feeling around inside the bag, she pulls out a blue asthma inhaler and takes two puffs from it. Rather than toss it back inside, she slips it in her pocket.

"When the humidity gets this bad it aggravates my asthma," Christina explains when she finds us all staring at her.

"We can slow down if that will help," Gal says in that protective voice that normally makes me smile.

"Thanks," she answers instead of trying to argue that it isn't necessary.

Don't get me wrong, I feel bad that she's having trouble breathing. My dad has asthma and sometimes he has to slow down to use his inhaler, too. It's just that I don't like where we are about to walk slowly by. We're near the Legare Mausoleum, which is still absent a certain lady ghost, and not so far beyond it will be the Raynor Mausoleum.

Before we left the chapel, I had kind of made up my mind to pass by it quickly. My thinking was that I could always seek Wade out later if I wanted to, as long as it's before dawn. Walking by it slowly will make it impossible for me to ignore the urge to look in that direction.

Not only that, but the others know about it now and I'm willing to bet all the money I *don't* have that they'll be curious to look as well.

I can't take the pressure anymore. We are so close to my family's crypt, it's just around the curve in the cemetery path ahead of us. I would rather risk the potential sight of other family ghosts' replaying memories than face my own.

I take the lead of our single-file line and veer us off the path and into the multitudes of family plots that I can already hear have conversations taking place from some pointless past. They are pointless to me anyway, I only care about avoiding my own at the moment.

Thankfully, no one in the line behind me says anything about my last minute decision to take the longer route to the front gate.

The section that proves impossible to dismiss is the sizeable orphan area. I don't care who you are, what's on your mind, how young or old you are, or where you came from and where you think you're going—it is not within the realm of the living to ignore children, living or dead, who are looking for their mothers. It does something to you that you never knew existed in your soul until that moment.

There's no way to save them, help them, or to know what became of them, and yet their misery is palpable beyond anything I could ever capture properly with words. You would just have to see and feel it for yourself, and I recommend to those who haven't, never to do so.

Sunny, Ava, and Gal are weeping helplessly while they attempt to reach all the children and send them away to end their sorrow. What they don't realize is that they are disturbing the memories and causing them more grief by not being able to answer their questions. There are simply too many of them.

Christina is standing beside me, stuck, like one of the cemetery statues. Not the grieving or hopeful kind, but one whose sculptor's hands left with a horrified expression. I nudge her hard to snap her out of it.

"Help me stop them," I tell her. She looks at me as though we have only just met, so I shake her and beg, "Christina, please!"

I don't know if she's having another asthma attack or what when she starts snatching at the shoulder straps of her backpack.

"You put your inhaler in pocket," I remind her.

She hesitates, and then a look of acuity clears the craziness from her expression.

"Okay, I'm sorry," she says and helps me convince the others to leave.

It's Gal that requires physical restraint. Only while I'm dragging him away do I realize—and gain new appreciation for—how much bigger and stronger he is than me.

When the crying babies, toddlers, and older children are finally out of audible range, I ask him if he's going to be okay enough for me to let go of the fistful of his t-shirt still clutched in my hand.

"Yeah, get off me," he bellows and shrugs me off as though my restraining him was more of a suggestion than an actual physical impediment.

We double-back through an avenue of live oak trees—the opposite direction of the front gate—until we are right back to where we started. I stare at the chapel doors and sigh my defeat at them.

It must be my lack of momentum that causes Ava to take my hand. She stands on her tiptoes to whisper in my ear, "Just get it over with, okay?"

I guess my dilemma is common knowledge after all. There is no way to avoid the Raynor Mausoleum without stumbling across some misery or another.

"I don't really have a choice," I think, but share the thought softly with her.

"You can choose to not listen."

Attempting to lighten the awful gloom I must be dumping on her, and Gal, and Sunny, and Christina— Shit!—and even myself, I grin a little and ask, "Will you get Gal to drag me away if I can't?"

"If my feminine persuasion fails me, then yes, I'll ask Gal to help me. Thank you, by the way, for getting me out of the orphan plot." I watch her shake her way too pretty head and listen intently while staring at her kiss-me lips say, "That was so horrible. The worst one yet."

"You're welcome. Yeah, I hated it, too."

I really did, but I assume the sound of my distracted voice is what makes Ava look up at me. Why do I like watching my thoughts being confirmed in her eyes? Maybe there's something inexplicably better about them trying to exist there. I've never thought about it before, but is it possible that someone else can make you better? Or rather, *want* to be better? If only I had given this more consideration before tonight.

"Payton!" There it is, the beautifully bashful smile that curves her lips and she knows how much I want to kiss them. She gives mine a chaste one and whispers, "Later, horny pants."

I may not have a *later*, but getting lost in Ava tonight has been a fulfilling enough lifetime for me. "Promise?"

She slides her hips against mine. "Yep."

Chapter Fifteen

My eyes are glued to the wet ground in front of me when we reach the path abutting the Raynor Mausoleum. For a moment, I try pretending the footsteps of the others didn't slow down. It is a denial I can't maintain when they come to a complete stop, though, and I have no other option but to raise my head.

Someone, I hope it's still Ava's fingers I feel, squeezes my hand. My gaze drifts toward the place they all have obviously already looked toward.

I'm struggling to remember whether or not I shut and locked my family's mausoleum door earlier today. Apparently, I didn't. It's wide open and standing in the doorway is my older brother. Seeing Wade hurts, seeing him dark and shimmering like the rest of the dead is an agony I'm not sure I will ever un-feel. I know he's watching me, but I can't acknowledge him yet.

If there is an honest bone in my body, I would admit that he is the reason why I'm here. I would also admit that he is why I couldn't carry out a rage-shooting.

His death was mine.

My suicidal thoughts are all born from the loss of Wade. He protected me from a dismal life of family expectations that I fear I'll fail to meet, or worse, be exceptionally good at. I need him back in my life, even if it's in the afterlife. I want to be with my brother again.

If Doc Fruitcake could hear my honest-for-once thoughts now, what would he diagnose me with?

Letting go of the hand in mine, I run to the nearest tree that offers a safe haven from further viewing of the single most important person to have ever lived and died in my pathetic life.

* * *

Though I can't recall how I got here, I'm suddenly cognizant of the wrought iron bars of the front gate. Ava is sitting beside me and Gal's stooped down on the bottom step of the old gatekeeper's building looking up at me. His lips are moving, but they don't quite sync up to the words I'm hearing.

"What?" I ask him and notice my jaw hurts.

"I said I'm sorry for hitting you." Gal winces and looks like he is expecting a reprisal he had already prepared himself for. "It was the only way I could calm you down."

"You went a little nuts when we tried to ask you what you wanted to do," Ava explains.

"I didn't hurt anyone, did I?" I scan everyone and they all look the same to me.

"No," Ava reassures me. "You were just really upset about seeing Wade and I was afraid you were about to run off again. So I asked Gal to help me. You know, like I said I would."

Her telling me this offers only a vague series of flashbacks where I'm fighting Gal with my fists, but losing. Reliving the last good memory of me, Wade, and our father is what's still fresh in my thoughts.

Dad had taken Wade and I to the Airforce base and surprised us with an up-close and personal view of a Marine V-22 Osprey. The crew was there for a one-day rest and refuel before continuing on with their flight plan.

Being a flight officer, and knowing the crew, Dad was able to get permission for Wade and me to tour one of them. We had played with a toy model of this aircraft constantly when we younger. It was amazing for us to actually be inside one and to feel the wash of those massive propellers during takeoff.

We had dinner with the crew that evening and I had my first taste of beer. Wade thought he was being slick, but Dad knew he swiped a mug and was keeping it on the floor between our chairs. Dad only smiled and pretended not to notice.

"It's okay, Ava, I'm not mad. Sorry I flipped out." I rub and stretch my jaw a few times. "Not bad, Gal. Didn't know you had it in you."

"I've never hit anyone before . . . I didn't like it."

"Forget about it."

Sunny and Christina move closer to the steps to get out of the way of a woman pushing a baby stroller with one hand while holding a parasol over her head with the other. She and stroller pass straight through the iron bars without the slightest hiccup.

"Well, if we were ghosts, we could leave," Sunny says.

Gal laughs. "Yeah, but could we drive a car?"

"So, are we gonna stay by the front gate till the caretaker shows up?" Christina asks.

"I think it's safest for all of us if we do. Who knows?" Gal shrugs. "If we're lucky, maybe the caretaker will show up early."

"What do you want to do?" Ava asks me. I know why she's asking.

"Gal's right," I say. "And you'll want the caretaker to see you right away instead of surprising him." I recognize my pronoun usage, particularly the lack of *we* so I switch subjects. "In a little bit I want to go back to the Raynor Mausoleum."

"Are you sure?" Gal asks, sounding doubtful.

"I'm sure." I give him a goofy expression for his benefit. "The shock of seeing him for the first time has already come and gone. I might be nervous, but I won't freak out again."

"All right, then." Gal stands up and looks inward toward the guts of Silentis. "Some rules first. We stick to the path, there and back. No ghost gazing, or conversations with ghosts thereof. Unless absolutely necessary, no touching of said ghosts."

"Lawyer brat."

Famous eye roll and then he says, "Army brat."

"We'll go in a minute," I say. "Let me just . . . I don't know, stand up, pace, breathe, think too much.

Maybe pop a valium." It's my attempt to be funny. He doesn't laugh.

"Oh, yeah, here." Gal opens his hand. "I already got one for you."

I frown at him when I stand. "You fished around in my pocket?"

"I wasn't playing pocket-pull, if that's what you're worried about."

Christina takes a seat at the step I had been sitting on next to Ava and watches her rummage through her backpack.

"What are you looking for?" Christina asks when Ava gets frustrated and starts dumping out the contents on the step below.

"There's a brush somewhere in this bottomless pit. I should've left my hair up, but since I didn't I have about a hundred knots now. Aha! Found it."

While she works the brush through her hair (yes, I'm watching because I find the simple act that mesmerizing), wincing with every tangle, Christina starts putting the items back in Ava's bag. "Whoa. You're not taking these, I hope. At least I hope you aren't relying on them anyway."

Me, Gal, and Sunny look at the thin, yellow pack Christina is holding up in front of her. A mixture of embarrassment and indignity forms on Ava's face. "Um, yeah." She sets the brush in her lap and takes the pack from Christina.

"Ava, those were recalled. Like, two months ago. Your pharmacist should've called you."

"What?"

"There was a huge fuck-up at the laboratory. The main component that makes them effective was missing. Seriously, though, didn't you get a call?"

I know Ava is trying to keep it together. She gets this look on her face that involves lots of blinking and you know she's clinching her teeth because her jaws flinch. Then her spine stiffens, making her sit up straight.

When she inhales that deeply controlled breath and holds it, I have no doubts she's working to keep herself from screaming a long list of obscenities. It's either gonna be that, or she'll string unrelated statements together in an unusually high voice.

"I got a new phone a while back. Upgrade and new number. I get mine filled three at a time because of my insurance. They should have sent me a letter in the mail. Email? Or something," she says in the high-octave voice. "Social media maybe!"

Lucky us.

"Don't they have your house phone number?"

"Hell no! I don't want my father to know I'm on the . . ." Ava glances at Gal, Sunny, and then her eyes lock with mine.

I sort out the obvious and I think Gal and Sunny do as well. They both look away and start talking about which graduation party is this year's must-attend. Since

153

Ava's new worries potentially involve me, there is no way in hell I'm going to turn away.

She turns back to Christina and asks, "Are you absolutely sure about this?"

"I'm positive." Christina taps the pack's front and continues, "This particular company is closed for now, but there are others who are picking up their slack. Who's your pharmacist?"

"The one your parents took over, Matthews Pharmacy." Ava is starting to look at Christina as though she's expecting her to fix the problem immediately.

"Christina, can you give us a minute, please?" I ask.

"Sure."

When she's gone, I sit down and put the rest of the things back in Ava's backpack. Once it's zipped up I lean in closer to her and say, "Try not to worry about it for now, okay?"

"Too late."

"Maybe nothing will happen." I feel woefully inadequate on the subject, but I know enough. I just don't want Ava worrying about it as much as I am. "It isn't like it's a done deal, right?"

She must have heard something resembling fear in my tone. "Right," she answers and nods too emphatically.

I want to tell her I'll be there for her no matter what, but that wasn't part of my plan to be there later. This is a crucial moment and I understand the importance of me saying something better than what's come out of my mouth so far.

"I know I've been an asshole to you for over a year now, and I'm so sorry for that." I take the brush from her lap and shove it in her backpack's side pocket. "You have always been important to me. I promise you that part never stopped."

"Thanks, Payton. I'm glad you told me that." She beams a smile at me and nudges my ribs. "Don't worry about this new situation. There are other options and I'll go to the pharmacy when they open later. Okay?"

"Okay."

"You ready?"

"Not really."

"Come on, I'll hold your hand."

And I take that offer, too.

We're just about to enter the path that will lead us to the Raynor Mausoleum when Ava stops to stare at one of the entry statues.

"What's up with this thing?" Ava asks. "I noticed it when we first got here."

"This is Saint Michael the Archangel," Sunny answers.

"Why is it so creepy?"

"It's not creepy." He looks at her as though she just exploded blasphemy all over us.

"But look." Ava points at the bottom of statue, where a figure struggles under Saint Michael's foot and nearing sword. "He's about to kill someone."

Sunny's expression softens.

"He's slaying Satan." His voice takes on that gentle tone you use when you're wanting to enlighten someone. Not in the passive-aggressive way, but when you truly want that person to come away with something—some greater knowledge than what they had before, or any if they had none at all. "He's a warrior who's saving heaven. Saint Michael also gives us a chance to redeem our souls at the hour of death, and he'll weigh all the souls on Judgment Day."

"Wow, Sunny," Christina says and turns from the statue to look at him. "Thanks for lesson. *Someone* paid attention during catechism classes." She nods at Ava. "I've always thought that statue was creepy, too. And I still do."

Chapter Sixteen

So we follow the path to the Raynor Mausoleum, and follow the rules. Ava is walking beside me, holding my hand, and Gal's to my right, not holding my other hand. Sunny leads the front of our group while Christina follows behind us.

At times, it isn't easy not to look. We are all guilty of breaking that rule, but haven't broken any of the others so far.

The one that really gets our attention is what we have slowed down for to enjoy without needing to okay it with each other first. We are watching, from our adhered-to position on the path, two entities of about twelve years old. There's a boy gently pushing a girl on a swing suspended from a tree branch that doesn't quite line up with the actual branch above them.

It is so glaringly evident they like each other and it's interesting to see how young courtship was a good century and a half ago. Most of it is the same, like how their laughter lilts and lasts a few seconds longer than it normally would if they were with anyone else. There's the delay, too, when her swing comes back to him and he holds it for a moment before sending her forward again.

Each time, she looks up at him wearing that expression girls must know from birth is the exact and most perfect way to look at a guy who's already nuts for you. It's mostly an angel's smile with a hint of something else locked up inside—and it is seductive in the captivating sense. We have zero chance of survival.

We watch him hold the swing for the longest time yet and listen to him ask her, "Jenny, are you going to the dance after church services this Sunday?"

"Yes. Are you?"

"Yes. I wanted to ask if you would save a dance for me."

"I would love to, John." Jenny lowers her voice, but we hear her say ever so demurely, "In fact, you may have them all."

John smiles from ear to ear and sends her swing forward again.

"That was entirely too precious," Gal says once we move past them.

"I know, right?" Ava leans forward to look at Gal from around me. "It was so sweet."

"Yeah, it was a great time," Christina grumbles from behind us. "Why are some of them so horrible? You'd think they would all want to relive only the good memories."

"Maybe some of them are stuck in a bad one." It seems plausible to me, especially when I consider the ones I get stuck in sometimes. "I'm sure us being here and getting in their way only makes matters worse."

"I've been thinking about that idea all night." Sunny stops walking and scans the area around us to make sure our conversation won't create any disturbances. "Like when we came across Mrs. White.

158

Her baby was already sick and what we saw may have been Mrs. White enjoying her last good day with the baby. Lots of babies died back then and she probably knew her baby wouldn't get any better. Where I'm going with this is there's a chance that when we interrupted her *good* memory, we brought out all the *bad* feelings she'd really been having."

"You're right, Sunny," Christina says. "It was me she passed through. I felt it when her memory shifted and I'd say her mood shifted with it."

"What about Mr. Shealy?" Gal asks.

"He was an asshole in life and in death." An expression of having just caught a whiff of fresh dog shit forms on Sunny's face. "No surprise there why he's a bigger asshole if you interrupt his fond memories of teaching his son how to torture women."

"But he grabbed me."

"Yeah, I don't have any ideas on that yet." Sunny shrugs. "Maybe he's an even bigger shit-head in the afterlife."

"Whatever," Christina dismisses the Mr. Shealy subject. "Personally, I think they're all getting stronger as it gets closer to dawn. What did that Legare woman say about the two we saw in the Greenhill section?"

"That perhaps they were from the *seat* of Silentis . . . whatever that means," I answer.

Christina groans her frustration and stomps off ahead of us. We scramble to catch up to her.

"Slow down," Sunny urges her. "What's wrong?"

"Nothing," she kind of barks, but slows her pace when what appears to be a butler ghost rushes ahead of her to open a door. "I'm so ready to get this night over with and be done with it already."

I find her choice of words to be a little off, and a lot annoying. What's there for her to be *done with*? If it weren't for the others I would question her. It's only now that I realize how many times I have wanted to question her since this whole thing started, but didn't.

"What school did you transfer from?" I ask her.

There is a slight delay before her clipped reply. "A private school in Hilton Head."

"Do you miss it?"

"You mean, did I like it better there than here at Charleston Harbor Prep?"

"Translate it however way you want to." I ignore the warning nudge Gal gives me and consider Christina lucky if I don't ask her if she had more friends there than she does here.

"I don't miss it or hate it, Payton, and here is just the same as there." Christina had yet to turn around since I started quizzing her about where she came from. To give her final assessment, though, she does and couples it with an all-inclusive sneer. "Same pompous bullshit, different city."

With no counterargument, I keep my mouth shut. She's right, but also wrong, in my opinion. Sure, there is no denying the ostentatious display of wealth and status here. I've never lived in Hilton Head, so I can't confirm nor dispel the amount of pageantry that goes on there. However, having lived here all my life, I find it hard to believe that pomp can get any more professional anywhere else.

The rest of the walk to the Raynor Mausoleum goes without further conversation. Somewhere along the way I stop looking up to see how close we're getting to it, choosing instead to keep my head down and preparing myself to see Wade again.

It's an infinitesimal movement among Ava's fingers, still intertwined with mine, that alerts me of not only our arrival to my family's tomb, but that Wade must still be there. I'm too terrified to lift my gaze from the ground.

"Payton," I hear Ava say before she stands in front of me. "Just look at him first and see how you feel before we go any closer."

Gal's hands go to my shoulders and gives me a reassuring mini-massage. More than likely, he is positioning himself to grab me should I run off again (clever boy). "He's watching us and he's so . . . um, clear, I guess. I don't know how to describe it, but it's not like the rest of what we've been seeing. Wade's not dark like them. He has light now, Pay."

Amazing, I get the nickname Gal used to call me when we were kids.

I'm trying to remember what I saw of Wade before I ran off earlier, but the only things that come to me are memories of him when he was alive. Gradually, because I'm still afraid, I lift my head and look at the mausoleum doorway.

And there he stands, my brother. Gal was telling the truth, Wade is full of light.

It reminds me of the light that appears in the other entities when we touch them, before they explode, when you can see a tiny bit more of their physical features. It's like Wade is anchored in that exact moment just prior to annihilation. To me, he looks like an angel. I'm not afraid anymore.

The loss of what everything Wade meant to me propels me forward to him. Nothing else in this world matters, only the opportunity that no one else ever gets—a second chance to tell someone who has died that you love them, that you miss them, and that your life is less than perfect without them . . . all that plagues the living mind.

It is not until I'm almost to him that I realize I've been crying. I pause, but only long enough to wipe my face dry.

"Wade," I say in more of a breath than aloud.

"Payton," his lips form my name.

I close the last of the distance between us and stand directly in front of him. What I wouldn't give to be able to hug him. He looks exactly as I remember and

I'm so thankful for that. "You're so much brighter than all the others," I say, then grimace at how silly it sounds.

"Am I?" Wade asks and examines himself. "Damn, check me out! Maybe I'm an angel. Do I have wings?" He turns a little to let me see his back.

Hearing my brother's still familiar teasing is a comfort that makes this whole day and night worth having woke up for. It occurs to me that the reason I enjoy Gal's humor so much, especially lately, is because it reminds me of Wade's.

"I miss you."

Wade faces me again. "I know. I feel it all the time. And I miss you, too, little brother." Rain starts falling, softly at first, then increasing with the addition of rolling thunder in the distance. "Better come inside," he says and glances over my shoulder at the others huddling themselves together under their towels. "Them, too."

When we enter the shelter of the Raynor Mausoleum, Wade and I go over to the statue of the phoenix rising from the ashes. Gal, Ava, Sunny, and Christina hang back near the entrance and talk quietly amongst themselves, no doubt out of respect for me and Wade.

I watch Wade's eyes drift upward to the inscription above the statue. "I'm not so sure about that. I feel pretty conquered."

"What's it like being dead?"

"Well, there's no beer and pizza." Wade's gaze leaves the inscription, settling for a moment on the phoenix, and then he looks at me. "There's no agony either, if that's what you're really asking." He hesitates briefly and I'm worried he may have more insight into my thoughts than I would prefer. I'm half-relieved when he asks, "How are Mom and Dad?"

"Fine." I shrug. It doesn't take much insight to know I'm lying and he sighs pointedly. I answer with the truth, "Mom's not doing well . . . you know how she gets sometimes. Dad? Well, he's who he is. The first few months after you died were really hard for him. He seems to be doing better lately." Obviously, I leave out *where* our father finds solace.

"He still tapping the neighbor?"

"You know about that?"

"Yeah." Wade looks disappointed. "Clearly, so do you, now. I'm sorry, Payton. When I was alive, I did everything I could to shield you from our father's extramarital affairs."

"*Affairs*?" I blurt out, but hushed-like so Ava doesn't hear. "As in plural?"

Nodding, Wade says, "As in I lost count when I was ten years old. It's like our dad was born with a hard-on and he'll probably go out with one. Saggy balls and all."

"Eww, that's gross." I dismiss the image of Dad's future old-man nuts. "Do you think Mom knows?"

"I never talked to her about it, but I think she knows about some of his affairs. I don't know why she chooses to look the other way."

Either the subject, or my unresolved issues with it, is starting to agitate me and I don't want to talk about Mom and Dad any more. The truth is I'm scared that if I lose it, Wade will vanish. I'm already worried that simply being too close to him could make it happen and when he takes a step closer to me, I take one back.

He frowns at me and it makes me sad to explain, "If I touch you, you'll go back."

"Oh." Wade's jovial smile returns. "So that's how it works?"

"That's how we've been doing it with all the other . . ." I'm not sure what to call them now that I'm talking to one who's my brother.

"Ghosts?" He laughs and it feels so good to hear it again. It's the circumstances that hurt me.

"Don't." I avert my eyes to the concrete floor and try not to think about how many Raynors could be roaming the catacombs beneath us.

Wade leans forward a little, taking more caution about keeping a decent distance now. "Hey, look at me." I do. "I know what's bothering you."

You could hear a pin drop on the concrete floor, but I ignore the others' sudden silence. "That's a lot of shit to know, Wade."

"You're worried you could turn out like Dad. Or worse, old man Levi."

The act of breathing becomes a job I have to work hard at. "It scares me more than you could ever understand." I must have voiced my thoughts aloud because I'm all at once aware of Wade's response. It comes rapidly and almost incomprehensible. "What are you saying?"

He slows down and repeats himself, "You're right to be scared. Be careful, Payton, you are capable of what you fear. Promise me you'll fight it."

Wade's being cryptic because of our audience, and it's also the Raynor way in such situations. But I know what he's warning me about and it is a painful reality hearing he thinks I have what it takes to keep the Raynor evil going.

"I am fighting it," seems about all I can say to him.

"Good." A bit of relief flits across his face. But it's not complete, like he's still deliberating on whether or not to say more on the subject.

"What?" I ask when he starts doing that nervous shifting from one foot to the other thing he always did when he was alive.

"I know what else is bothering you." Even in death, I can tell when Wade is stressing out. It's a little like how I react, but not as intense. "My death wasn't your fault. You have to stop blaming yourself for it. *I* need you to stop."

Chapter Seventeen

If you could hear a pin drop before, you should hear the way it bounces. The others toss their manners aside and inch forward, stopping short of a few feet directly behind Wade. If he hadn't have touched on a sensitive subject for me, I would call them out on it.

"What happened?" I ask. "You were talking to me one minute and then you yelled and I heard screeching sounds . . . and then there was nothing."

"Someone ran me off the road."

This revelation threatens my resolve to keep my stress level in check. "What? Who?"

"I don't know. There was a car following close behind me for a while. I thought the driver meant to pass me, but when the car got alongside mine it slammed into me. The last memory I have is seeing the trunk of that oak tree."

Wade's car had been such a crumpled pile of twisted metal, it was assumed all the damage came from the impact. The condition of his body matched that of the car. We were told his death was instant, that there was no suffering. But I have suffered every day since then.

"Did you see who was driving the other car?" My heart and head is pounding.

"Not really. I got a glimpse, enough to know there was only one person in it. Everything happened so fast."

"Dammit!" I'm so close to snapping. I have to close my eyes for a second to concentrate on the singularity of calm.

"Payton, you need to calm down. Okay?"

"No, Wade. We never knew why you ran into that tree. I always thought it was because you were talking on the phone with me and not paying attention. Now you're telling me that someone purposefully ran you off the road. Someone killed you, Wade. Do you know of anyone who would've wanted to hurt you?"

"I can't imagine—" Wade's eyes bulge, and I'm thinking he may have remembered something. But he looks down at his torso, and so do I, and we both see a hand protruding through his abdomen. "What's happening to me?"

Instead of gaining a light, Wade is slowly fading away. The hand that so callously causes his second departure from me belongs to Christina. He is confused at first, but then I suppose he remembers what I told him because he swings back around to me.

"I don't care about any of it." He's talking rapidly again. "I love you, Payton. Remember what I said, fight it."

"I love you, too," I whisper as the last of him dissipates.

I'm left standing here, again. Feeling numb, again. Staring through the space where Wade had been, again.

My eyes refocus and fix on Christina. "You bitch! Why'd you do it?"

In this most vengefully felt moment, what I would like to do is choke the life out of her—quite slowly in fact. Images of me doing just that arrange themselves for my mental viewing pleasure. Resisting the impulse to carry out the fantasy, I glory in the genuine fear expressed in her eyes instead. It is a vicious pleasure for me to have caused it.

"I'm sorry. I was afraid that you were getting upset. You know, like you did earlier."

Now, I'm not a puny guy, but Gal is huge. He could have easily been a quarterback if he felt so inclined to try out for the football team.

It's intimidating when he positions himself in front me and braces my shoulders with his big hands, preventing me from getting around him so I can continue my visual assault of Christina. I get a firm shaking for my efforts to wrestle free from his grip.

"Stop it!" Gal gets right up in my face, forcing our eye contact, and he doesn't soften his hold on me until he sees he has my full attention. "Breathe, relax, let it go."

I swear on everything holy and not, he could be a Yoga class instructor, too, if he wanted. Gal's hypnotic nodding and swaying actually does have a calming effect on me. I'm not sure at what point I begin mimicking his movements, all I know is that I'm finding myself to be a good little charmed cobra.

Where is the anger I had for Christina's stupid insensitivity? I have no idea, ask Gal where he put it.

"I'm fine, now," I tell him. Gal raises a manicured eyebrow at me, as though I'd better not bullshit a bullshitter. "Seriously, it's done. I swear, it's over. I'm not gonna yell at her anymore."

"All right." Gal looks like he's thinking about something. I find out what it is during the big bear hug I'm engulfed in. "I'm glad you know it's not your fault, but I hate what we know now." He leans back and lets me go. "Maybe your dad can get the case reopened so they can catch whoever did this to Wade."

"What am I supposed to tell him? Wade's ghost told us someone purposefully ran him into a tree? He'll think we're crazy, or on drugs . . . which we are."

"Well, just think about it."

* * *

Though the rain has stopped, it may as well be pouring still with all the humidity it left behind. Five minutes after leaving the Raynor Mausoleum, Christina stops to use her inhaler. I feel guilty for yelling at her and calling her a bitch now that I've calmed down.

I mean, I'm still pissed she made it her personal duty to rid me of my brother, but it's not her fault how I overreact to stressful situations sometimes.

"We can stop and rest as many times as you need," is my best way of apologizing to her.

"Thanks," is Christina's best way of accepting it.

I'm not sure why, but I really want to be near Ava. I turn and find her only a few feet away, smiling at me. She must have heard my attempt to be nice to Christina.

Her hair is all frizzy again and her clothes are filthy. So are everyone's. Either the rain, or exhaustion, has smeared the make-up beneath her eyes, but she looks hideously beautiful to me. I don't care who is watching us, my lips on hers are what I want and that's what happens when I pull the full length of her body against mine. As much as I want to, I do control the urge to lead Ava to the nearest private obelisk.

"Hey, hormones," Gal calls over to us. "If you're done making the rest of us wish we had someone to snog with, can we go now?"

I feel Ava's lips smiling against mine. If your lips have never felt someone else's lips smiling, I highly recommend putting it on your list of things to experience before you die. It's a beautiful feeling.

Reluctantly, I pull back and hate the way the introduction of air feels between our bodies.

* * *

We have to ease around a family plot in full swing of no less than three ghostly generations. Sunny is in the middle of explaining that he had read the plot's main headstone earlier and how the whole family had died during the big Charleston earthquake of 1886 at an annual family reunion.

We've yet to express our typically shocked horror for such a tragedy when Ava's hand is yanked from mine. Her scream and sudden disappearance takes a couple of seconds to register before I panic.

"Ava!" I shout and Gal grabs my arm before I fall in the same hole she went down.

"Payton!" Ava's terrified voice yells up from the bottom of the freshly dug grave. "What happened? Where am I? I can't see anything."

Gal and I flatten out on the ground. "Ava, you fell in a grave," I say and consider only afterward that I probably should have said *hole* instead.

I wait to hear if she's going to freak at the news, but all she says is, "Oh, shit."

"Are you hurt?"

"I don't think so," she answers up to us. There's nothing for a second, then, "Please get me out of here. I'm scared."

"I'll have you back up before you know it," I promise her.

Without a *'May I?'*, *'Please'*, or even, *'Thank you'*, I snatch everyone's towels off their shoulders and start tying them together long ways.

Some weird, primitive instinct kicks in— probably an archaic, caveman-like flashback of wanting to save what I perceive is my woman. I almost shove Gal and Sunny away when they figure out what I'm planning and try to help me. Thankfully, I don't do that and end up relying on their help since my hands are shaking and making a mess of securing the knots properly.

We're almost finished when Christina comes over and kicks aside one of the two-by-fours that had been stretched across the opening. "Shouldn't this have been covered better?"

"Since no one is supposed to be in here at night, they're only concerned about things like raccoons and possums falling in," Gal answers. "There's probably a funeral taking place today and the grave is usually dug the day before."

"OH SHIT!" Ava screams, and what sounds like her hands patting frantically against the wet dirt walls accompanies her next words. "Hurry, please, hurry up. Something else is down here. I can feel it. Oh, God, I can hear it."

It's all I can do to stay calm and I find success by being the voice of calm. "We made a rope from the towels. I'm gonna lower the looped end down to you and we'll pull you up. I want you to put your foot in the loop and hold on, okay?"

"Okay."

We lower the rope. "You got it?"

"Yeah."

There's not much towel left to pull her up with, so we settle on a human-pulling-human chain technique. Gal is behind me with his arms tucked under mine and I can hear him grunting, and farting. Sunny and Christina are tugging on both of us while I dig my heels into the soggy ground and pull Ava from a grave I'm determined won't be hers.

I take my first breath of hope at seeing her hands reach over the top of the hole and claw at the mud by my shoes. Letting go of the towel rope to help her the rest of the way is not an option so I point the toes of my shoes forward for her to find.

When she does, Gal must have been watching and waiting for this exact moment with me, because I'm pretty sure I only help him by holding the rope while he yanks us both backwards.

Ava is out, but crying like she's just seen Satan himself and listened to him whisper nothing but unspeakable horrors in her ear on her way up. I take a quick scan of her to make sure she's in one whole unbloodied piece.

When I'm satisfied the sobs are not the result of physical pain, I wrap my arms around her and pull her to my chest so she can cry it out there in private.

Eventually, I employ a recent lesson learned from Gal and sway with her. It takes a bit longer, but Ava finally relaxes. Again, I hate the air between us when she gathers herself together enough to sit up. It feels better when she needs me, I think. Or, maybe, it's that I need her, I have to consider . . . confess.

It starts raining again and this time it's a good thing, even with the lightning and thunder it brought along for company. Not only is it rinsing the outer layer of mud off of us, the rumbling din provides the perfect opportunity for Ava to lean over me and say, "I've loved you for so long, you dumb-ass."

At least I hope that's what she just said. While my fingers mean only to caress, they also succeed in replacing one streak of mud on her cheek with a new one, and I say, "I love you, too, Ava. Always, you."

"Come on, let's get away from here." She stands and holds out her hands to help me up.

I can feel my plans and grand schemes crumbling beneath me. It is in this moment that Ava could suggest following her back down that hole and I would follow her there without question.

As I'm standing, I hear Sunny say something about using the towel rope to get over the gate. Out of my peripheral vision, I see that Christina is standing on it, but turns to say what a great idea this is and when she steps away it falls into the hole—hopelessly out of our reach.

Who cares? It's all a vague reality to me and I just wish they'd both shut the hell up so I can continue to perch on the edge of whatever else Ava might say.

Gal to the rescue once more, sort of. He puts a quick end to Sunny and Christina's bickering, only not with his typical way of getting it done.

"Shut the fuck up! Sunny, just forget about the damn rope, we'll be out of here soon enough anyway. Christina, stop pissing people off."

That gets my attention. I break eye contact with Ava and look at Gal to see he is already working on regaining his composure, mud and all.

"You guys want to stop by the chapel before we head back to the gate?" I ask.

Of course, everyone is all about visiting the chapel's bathroom. If for no other reason than to clean the filth from our hands and faces.

Also, I'm certain the shut bathroom door provides a quiet moment for each of us to be alone with our vulnerabilities.

Chapter Eighteen

On the way to the front gate, we revert back to Gal's initial rules and remain absolutely quiet the whole time, ignoring all things not of this living world. Once we're back, the humidity is less oppressive in the more open space of the grand cemetery entrance. It lurks amongst the oak trees and saturated headstones instead like a menacing villain ready to pounce should we venture inside.

Interestingly, I don't care about being secretive anymore where Ava's concerned. If I'm not holding her hand, I've got my arm wrapped around her. Regardless if anyone is looking or not, I kiss her when I can't not kiss her any longer. The only thing I won't do is take her clothes off, though I desperately want to.

"I'll be right back."

I start to let go of her hand, but she clamps her fingers tightly onto mine. "Where are you going?"

"To pee," I answer. She frowns at me. "I didn't have to go earlier while I was taking a sink bath. But it's hitting me now and I'd rather not piss my shorts."

"Oh."

Damn if she doesn't look up at me with that expression. "I'm just going around the back. Save my seat?"

Ava stretches her legs out on the step. "I will, if you promise to think about me."

"That's an easy promise to make."

So, while I'm taking a piss, I sort of hope I'll see her come around the side of the gatekeeper's house. She doesn't, though, and that gives me time to think. I stare absentmindedly at the white wood planks siding the building while thoughts of how bizarre the last . . . Jesus! What time is it now?

Getting the last out in impatient squirts, I stuff 'let's-go-visit-Ava' back in my shorts and check my phone. It's 4:08 a.m. and some of the air from my happy balloon escapes.

Besides the quick nap in the chapel, it has been almost twenty-four hours since I slept and woke up to start this crazy-ass last day of mine. Yes, a lot has changed, but much remains the same.

I reflect back over parts of the conversation Wade and I had. It's depressing as hell to know Wade thinks—thought, *whatever*—that I have in me what it takes to be a true Raynor. I told him I'd fight it and I haven't changed my mind about how to win that battle. It is the only way I know how to win it.

This night has truly been the weirdest of my life thus far, and it's also been the greatest. I've come a long way, too. A day ago I had it in my head that I wanted to kill people before taking myself out. Remembering that—acknowledging it—shames me now.

Had I been teamed with different people, I might have done it. I'll never know and I'm glad I won't. I want to go out of this life knowing I've never killed anyone. That's part of what makes Raynors so evil and what makes them excel in the military. They (we) kill people without flinching.

When I was about nine years old, I heard my grandfather telling a story of the first time he killed someone. He said it was the only time it had been difficult, but that it turned out to be the most thrilling because subsequent killings became somewhat boring from then on.

He likened it to losing his virginity, saying that though sex was one of his favorite activities, he would never forget how perfectly awkward and perfectly electrifying his first conquest was. He had gone on with other *firsts*, none of which I care to mention. All I'll say is that they became progressively worse in the inhuman sense.

I've wasted too much time thinking about that horrible man, I think I'll spend the last of my time with Ava. I glance at my phone again and see there are two additional voice messages from my father since the last one.

Like the first one, I'm not going to listen to these either. For a moment, I think about tossing the phone over the wall. It's not like I can take it with me, right? Ultimately, I decide not to and tuck it back inside my book bag.

Just before I reach the side of the building to go back out front, I stop short of running through an entity who's standing there blocking my way.

"There is evil here," he says to me.

Assuming he means me, I tell him, "Not for much longer."

"I'm not talkin' 'bout you, boy, though I'm not pleased with the sins you have committed in my chapel. Fornication in a house of God isn't Christian-like behavior . . . especially outside the sanctity of marriage."

It's only now that I realize he's clutching a bible to his chest, giving it a firm pat as though the proof lies within the bound pages. I'm confused about the evil reference he made initially, but can't let slip the opportunity to point out the obvious.

Matching his ridiculous Southern brogue, I say, "I don't suppose it's Christian-like behavior to watch fornication in a house of God either."

"Payton, what's taking you so long?" Ava comes from around the side and also just barely misses traipsing through the Reverend. "Oh, another ghost, huh?" She scoots by with as much distance between him and the hedge as she can muster.

"Actually, Ava, this is Reverend Ghost." Ava takes my hand and tries not to giggle. I haven't a clue what she finds so amusing. "He was just telling me that you and I are fornicators."

"Oh, really?" Ava sneers at him. "May I have the pleasure?" She asks me and lifts her hand toward the entity.

"Wait," Reverend Ghost says. "Your sins can be forgiven."

I can almost see where this is going. "How's that?" I ask anyway.

He speaks directly to Ava. "Allow me to marry you."

"Are you crazy?" She scoffs at Reverend Ghost. "I'm not marrying you."

"He means *us*, Ava." I'm trying not to giggle myself. "The Reverend is just asking for your permission."

"Shouldn't it be *you* asking for my permission?"

"Well?"

"Well what?"

"You want to?"

"Payton, are you being serious?"

"Come on, it'll make him happy and then you can send him off." She's shooting me a dubious look, so I add, "It's the least we can do for fornicating in his chapel."

Ava finally gives in to the fit of laughter her giggles had wanted to be. Then she waves her hand at the Reverend and says, "Okay."

* * *

"Geez, you guys are like rabbits," Gal says when Ava and I come back to the front of the gatekeeper's house. "You could at least offer to let me watch." His eyes scan us from head to toe and then his nose crinkles. "Nah, on second thought, never mind."

"We just got ghost-married," Ava announces.

"You did what?" Gal moves over so we can pass by and sit on the top step.

"Yeah, it seemed the chapel's Reverend Ghost's eternal happiness depended on him joining us in holy matrimony to make right," Ava leans forward to whisper the rest into Gal's ear, "our sinful fucking."

"Did he say that?"

"No, he kept calling it *fornicating*."

Gal snorts. "Good Lord. I wonder what he'd call the things I do."

"The devil's influence?" I suggest.

"That would imply that Satan is gay. Maybe that's why hell is all aflame." Gal explodes into laughter at his own joke. When he's over himself, he asks, "How did he know anyway?"

"Apparently, he's a peeping pastor," I answer. "He probably hoped for absolution of his own perverseness by seeing to it that we weren't sinners anymore."

"Well, congratulations. You think it's legally binding?"

"Yeah, sure, Gal," Ava frogs his arm, "in 1860-something Payton and I are Mr. and Mrs. Rabbit."

"Heads up, you guys," I call out to Christina and Sunny, who have been standing by the front gate since we got back.

They turn and scramble out of the way of several entities intending to leave Silentis. Unfortunately,

Christina isn't fast enough with one of them. The elderly lady, who is wearing an elaborate hat decorated with flowers and giant feathers, passes through her. She yells at Christina for panhandling until the imploding light silences her.

"I'm looking forward to pretending like this night never happened," Christina says on her way over to us.

Something in her tone bothers me. For one thing, she sounded pretentious just then, kind of like she thinks we're all beneath her in some way. It doesn't match my perception of her—the meek, friendless girl that Christina leads everyone into believing she is.

Not even twenty-four hours ago I viewed her in that same light, but there is definitely something about her that either evolved tonight, or was always there.

"Is that easy for you? Pretending shit doesn't happen?" I ask her.

"Sometimes," she answers. "It depends on the subject. Some things you can't pretend out of existence."

"It won't be much longer," Sunny says while gazing at the front gate longingly.

Christina continues staring at me and says, "No, it won't." A smile curves her lips and I swear on everything I know that there is something both familiar and wicked lurking in her eyes right before she shifts back to shy mode. "Right?"

I ignore her.

"Is the street still flooded, Sunny?" I ask.

"Yep," he answers. "But it looks like the water is starting to recede now."

"I keep thinking about that girl in the Greenhill section." Ava's brushing through a section of her hair, still grimacing whenever she hits a particularly stubborn tangle and I still like watching her brush her hair. "Think I could pull off that hairstyle, Gal?"

"Yeah . . . no." Gal chuckles when Ava smacks his shoulder with the brush. "Why are you asking me anyway? It's because I'm gay, isn't it? Ya' know, not all gay men are hair stylists."

"And not all male hair stylists are gay, Gal."

"Touché."

"I thought you didn't know French."

"*Is* that French?"

"My water is all hot and gross now," Christina interrupts the banter and dumps out the dregs from her bottle. "Give me all of yours and I'll refill them while I'm doing mine."

Gal pours his out, too, and hands it over. "I'll have the mocha latte flavored parasitic water, please."

Christina laughs and waits for the rest of us to hand over ours. "Need any help?" Sunny asks.

"No. I'm just going over to the spigot around the side. I'll be right back."

When she turns the corner, I whisper, "You guys find anything off about her?"

"A little," Ava admits. "Maybe she's just socially awkward."

"She's definitely not consistent," Gal adds his opinion. "Her personality and the way she reacts to things are all over the place."

"I noticed that, too, that's why I asked." I shrug it off, though. It's possible she sees Dr. Mead for more problems than what she mentioned to me.

"I've seen her watching you a lot," Sunny says to me. "It could be she has a crush on you."

Though I find it odd she's been watching me, I don't think it's because of that reason. When I got too close to her the first time we were in the Raynor Mausoleum, she moved away. Rather quickly, I had noticed. She almost seemed repulsed by the idea that I might touch her. I hardly know her and I can't fathom a reason why she would be watching me.

While I'm trying to sort through potential scenarios, Gal and Ava give me a simultaneous nudge.

"Thank you, Christina," Gal says and takes the water bottle she extended toward him. He stares at it suspiciously. "This one is mine, right? God only knows where Payton's mouth has been."

She smiles, the shy kind, and answers pretty much the same way, "Yeah, I made sure I didn't get them mixed up."

Everyone chugs from their rightful bottles after she diligently makes a point to title the rest with our names during the process of handing them over.

It's impossible for me to not keep glancing over at her after what Sunny told me. In my opinion, she seems far more interested in Sunny, Gal, and Ava.

The only other thing I notice about her, and struggle to remember if I'd seen her doing it before, is how she constantly fidgets with her glasses.

Naturally, this is when Christina shifts her attention to me—when I'm frowning and trying to sort out what the hell it is she's doing to her glasses. She stops immediately and for a tiny second, her gaze settles on the pen in my front shirt pocket before she sits down on the bottom step.

There is not one reason I can come up with that would explain the coincidence, but I sincerely hope there is one. If she knows what it really is, then why hasn't she called me out on it by now?

Chapter Nineteen

The first to yawn is Gal. He stretches his long legs out on the step and props his head back between two of the wooden porch railings.

The uncomfortable look of comfortable enough prompts Sunny to follow Gal's example, but it takes him longer to situate the back of his head in the crook of the two railings. He yawns several more times and mumbles something about not letting him nap longer than some-odd minutes before closing his eyes.

Christina eyes them both and lets go her own yawn, a bit overdone in the joining of the crowd way in my opinion. Rather than mimic their chosen way of resting on porch steps, she lays down on her side, facing outward toward Silentis, and uses her backpack for a pillow. I can't see her face from the top step Ava and I are sitting on, but I hear Christina yawn pointedly again then proceed with a few last wiggles for unattainable comfort.

When she seems to have settled, I still wait another minute or so before attempting to talk to Ava. I glance over at Gal and smile at how funny he looks asleep. His mouth is slightly open and I can just hear the beginning of what will turn into a full-blown snoring session.

Sunny, on the other hand, is completely silent. His mouth is closed, but he does twitch a lot and it reminds of when you see puppies sleeping.

Quietly, I point at them, but Ava's head doesn't move from where it took up residence leaning against my shoulder. I look down and find her asleep as well, her hand still holding the brush in her lap. I'm only mildly disappointed that she's not awake, as I had hoped to spend my very last seconds enjoying her company.

Though, now that I think about it, I won't have to make up excuses for why I don't need anyone to come with me to retrieve the camera I *accidentally* left at the chapel.

It doesn't matter whether she's asleep or awake, I can enjoy her company either way. I move her head to my chest, because I want to know what that feels like, too. It feels great (like all of it has) and I imagine it would feel even better if we were in a bed.

You were the only one who made me consider not doing it. That's what keeps floating around in my head while I spend my time avoiding the look of the night sky initiate the first changing of the colors.

At this point, I don't want her to wake up and that's why it takes me so long to pull the notebook out of my backpack so I can write that thought down. I scribble away at the rest of my thoughts to her and look it over before committing to tucking it away in her bag.

> *Dear Ava,*
> *First, please know that you were*
> *the only one who made me consider*
> *not doing it. But I have to do it. I*

have to end this potential for evil that I know is locked up inside of me. I'm out of the equation now. Trust me, the world is a better place without Raynors. Don't waste your time with regret. There was nothing you, or Gal, could have done differently that would have changed the outcome. You stepped out from the shadows I banished you to and made my last night less dark. You're a beautiful person, Ava. Live a good life.
I leave loving you,
Payton

* * *

The jacket I didn't need on this sweltering night provides the pillow I rest Ava's head on. She stirs a little when I stand up, and for a moment, I'm worried her eyes will open. But they don't.

It's hard for me because I kind of hoped they would and that she'd somehow know what I'm about to do, and that she'd find a way to stop me by offering a solution I hadn't thought of. I prove that hope to myself when I risk leaning down to gently kiss her lips. Perhaps I should have put more passion into it because she continues sleeping.

I turn away from her, from the sight of her. That's the only way I can deal with it. It turns out, taking my last visual of Gal is just as hard on me and I avert my eyes away from him even more quickly.

Carefully, I step over and around all of them and reach the bottom of the steps. I want to look back at them, but I know better. To look at them would make the act of killing myself a screaming reality that I simply cannot acknowledge right now.

To ensure I haven't disturbed anyone, I pause to listen for motion with every couple of steps I take away from them and into Silentis' surreal. After a while, well past that certain distance where I know they wouldn't be able to see me even if they did wake up and notice my absence, I stop pausing.

Wade told me this story a long time ago of the most talked about legend of Silentis. We were kids, I think Wade was twelve and I had just turned nine, and our whole family was at the cemetery for our great-grandmother's funeral.

Of course, unable to fully relate to death at that time, we were bored and entertaining ourselves while the adults mused amongst themselves about how great a lady Evelyn Raynor was. We listened to the occasional comment about how not-so-great the Legares were, but the reality is that the Raynors have always had a secret boner for the Legares.

After pulling me aside, Wade pointed up at a tree branch where at least a dozen bluebirds perched. They were lined up side by side and each one seemed to be watching the congregation of Raynor family mourners below.

For a nine year old boy, I thought they looked sweet enough to admire a while until Wade explained what their purpose for being there was.

"There's an Indian chief buried somewhere in here in an unmarked grave and he tells the birds to stay near where the next person to be buried will go," he had said. We both eyed the bluebirds in a newly suspicious light. Wade added in a whisper, "And they have to stay there for the first whole day so that the dead person won't be scared on their first night in Silentis."

I have never forgotten that conversation. I'm sure it's total bullshit, but it is a cool story, right? Remembering it helps me as I pass through a multitude of entities on my way to the chapel, the place I've decided is the most poignant of all to end my life.

Accurate description defies me at trying to explain what's happening around me the closer I get to the chapel. It's like the ghosts are amassing in a sort of last minute chance to provide a glimpse of what their living world was really all about to the one who is still technically alive. I almost can't wait to be dead so as not to be haunted by them anymore.

"Don't do it," I hear a man's raspy whisper from behind me. "You could always just run away, boy." Hell stands a better shot at freezing over twice before I would turn around to acknowledge him.

I'm not sure if this entity is talking to me or not, but I have thought about it. Many times, as a matter of fact. Despite all the Raynor family money, I, Payton Raynor, have zero dollars. Where the hell would I go? The streets? Like I know anything about how to live like that. I'd be dead by the end of the week. Even if I somehow managed to survive, old-man Levi would have me found and forcibly drug back home.

The last of the torment comes in the form of an abrupt silence that threatens my resolve to not look over my shoulder to see if the ghosts are really gone. I'm just about to do it anyway when an entity materializes right in front of me, forcing me to stop or else go through him.

"This last day does not belong to you," he says to me.

I don't want to reply and I'm super pissed off that I have to come up with some way of getting past this new monolithic presence. I'm contemplating touching him so I can be on my way. As I lift my hand to be done with it, he confuses me by doing the same. Finally, I look up into his eyes to find amused curiosity. When a frown forms on his face, and he tilts his head to the side, I realize he is mirroring my own expressions.

My irritation explodes into anger. "Dude, what the fuck is wrong with you?" I yell. "Get away from me."

"Do as you wish, Payton. Go to the chapel if you must. I only want you to know that the birds perched there are not waiting for you."

Though he hasn't said all that much, I've heard and had enough of him. I ram my fist through the middle of him with imperfect, yet still deeply satisfied, pleasure. I decide that I'll expend what little time I can afford to watch this annoying beast of a giant dissolve.

The only problem is that he's not doing so by way of my command, but of his own accord. It seems his departure-preference is of the slow and taunting variety. I get the feeling that he's waiting patiently for what words I may happen to give before he will exit completely.

Fine. I know exactly what I want to say to him. "This is *my* life. I own it, and I control it. It's mine to live, and it's mine to die."

"Very true." His fading head nods. "All in good time, Payton Raynor."

And then he's gone. Rather than a light building to an explosion, he disappears into a miniscule version of one, almost a reverse pattern of what I've been seeing all night. There is no time for me to think it over because his replacement shows up within seconds.

Lucky me.

"We mek fuh de chu'ch, now, suh. Dem bu,ds bin hol'n on fuh de nyew plateye."

It's the same man that was in the chapel earlier. "I thought we sent you back," I say to him.

"A wu'k all ob'duh chu'chyaa'd. Sen me'way fom one place, A sho op een anudduh."

I can't be mean to him, not like I was with the other entity. I doubt he knows that it's only been a few years since the church massacre.

It was so horrible. If you ever want to sadden a room full of Charlestonians, just bring the subject up. I know I take some nasty jabs at Charleston, and some of them are well-founded, but I can't deny the united comradery that exists here.

Shitty stuff still happens, always has and always will, but we unite quite easily and naturally. Outsiders are welcomed with open arms and giant smiles. Take an open, giant shit on us and you'll even see forgiveness.

But do it again? Hospitality becomes a twisted bastard, with still-open arms and still-giant smiles, but with eyes now scrutinizing your every move—enhanced by hindsight and every good reason—to publically shame you should your farts stink worse than low tide.

"No peace for you either then. Not even in death, huh?" I suddenly feel like a rotten piece of shit for comparing my life (or impending afterlife) to his. "What's your name?"

"Abram, suh."

"Well, Abram, suh, I'm on my way to the chapel now. You don't need to come with me, but thank you for offering." To make sure he doesn't argue with me, and I feel bad for tricking him, I extend my hand and say, "It was nice meeting you."

He only realizes what I've done a split second after his hand reaches mine. "Oona ceebe me." Abram doesn't seem overly mad about it. Before he goes, he adds, "Git along, now, an tek'care yasef, suh."

When he's gone, I pass through what I assume is the last labyrinth of diminishing ghosts. Then Silentis turns silent. I am truly alone now. It is a lonely place I'm used to.

As I get closer to the chapel, my pace slows while I think about the dead. In some ways they never really die. Everything they ever were is still there, day after day—haunting us in a quiet way. It's everything they never became that tortures most people.

For me, that's Wade. His death punched a hole in my life. That hole grew into a hollow that is now a lonely cavern where, '*Why did you leave me?*' echoes because I shout it all the time in my head.

Wade was always my big brother. I was always his, 'little bro.' When he died, he not only took his protectiveness over me with him, he also left with my very definition. I don't know what I am anymore. I don't know who to be, what to be, or how to be it.

I push these thoughts aside before they trap me inside my own mind. Willing myself forward, I start running the rest of the way to the chapel.

Chapter Twenty

My running to get here faster comes to a skidding halt when I do. I stare blankly at the unexpected sight that greets my eyes for a minute or so. A shit-ton of birds are perched on the chapel roof, in the nearby trees, loitering around the front and sides, and generally just everywhere.

Nope, they are not cute little bluebirds either. Turkey vultures, that's what I get!

Whoever the Indian chief is that's in charge of this bird-myth, clearly must not like Raynors either. That, or he has a fantastic sense of humor.

These birds are so dorky. I'm watching two of them in the middle of what looks like an ongoing debate over where a stick should be placed on the ground.

It's laughable. If it were anybody else, I would laugh. I have to walk through a group of them to get to the front door and half of them follow me.

"No," I say to one when it tries going inside with me. "Stay out here with your, um, friends?"

After shutting the door, I lean against it and scan every surface of the chapel's interior. I'm not sure where I should do it and I feel kind of guilty about the mess I'll probably make.

An image of Abram with a mop instead of a broom pops into my head. It's macabre enough that I consider shooting myself outside. Unfortunately, I hadn't been expecting a committee of vultures and I'm more than sure a gunshot would create instant chaos.

I push off from the door and head down the center aisle. Once I'm settled in the first pew next to my camera, I flip through all the images we took. I linger longest on the ones of Ava.

Maybe I'm just wasting time, but I pull out my laptop and upload the images from the camera, the data from the pen, and all of what I had been transferring to my phone whenever I got the chance.

It seems woefully inadequate to me so I spare (and waste) more time to update my not-so-manifesto of a high school shooter. Apparently, I didn't have it in me after all. I'm okay with being this kind of a failure, I don't want to kill people.

I suppose it's just a suicide note now. Jesus! Do they ever come this detailed? It occurs to me that the pool of information will leave as big of a mess as the pool of my blood will.

There is one last thing I want to do. I've decided to listen to my father's voice messages.

"Payton, I need to talk to you. Call me as soon as you can."

His worried tone is one I recognize easily, having heard it constantly when Wade died. Several thoughts come to me, but I fear the possibility that he may have found the note I left for my mother. I'm not too keen on listening to the next two messages and while

I'm contemplating whether or not I should, the second one starts playing automatically.

"Where are you and why haven't you called me back yet?" Anger has crept into his voice, but I still hear the worry. *"It's important and I'd rather not say it in a message. Please call me."*

Now I'm worried.

The third message begins with an exhausted sigh. *"I have no idea why you won't return my calls, son."* He clears his throat and sighs again. *"Your mom is in the hospital. When I got home from work . . . I found her. I couldn't wake her up. She overdosed. It was touch and go for a while, but her doctors say she's going to pull through it. I'm staying with her tonight, so call the hospital when you get this message. I hope you're all right, Payton."*

But I'm not all right.

My mom is an expert at knowing how much of what to take and exactly which pill pairs best with a red or a white wine. I know she found my letter. Losing two sons and definitive proof that at least one son knew of her husband's adultery was too much for her.

If there's a bright side to be had (believe me, I'm struggling to find one and hold on to it) it's knowing that my father still cared enough to want to save her. Maybe she'll get the help she needs, and maybe they'll work on their marriage. I really hope so.

I shove the camera, the laptop, and the phone inside my backpack and take the gun out. Before zipping it closed, I retrieve the spare mag and put it in my shorts pocket. I would rather have the weapon and all the ammunition found on my body. The coroner will secure it properly. No need to risk letting it fall into the wrong hands, like mine for example.

I'm not sure why I brought so many bullets with me. Even if I shot the others before turning the gun on myself, there would still be ten rounds left in the gun to kill us twice more. With the extra mag, I could shoot our ghosts three more times.

A rush of relief sweeps over me that I didn't kill anyone. I may not have had it in me today, but *would* I with enough tomorrows? When I think about Gal and Ava—and, yes, even Sunny and Christina—I feel sick to have entertained the idea.

Does this mean there is still some semblance of good inside of me? Was my grandfather always an evil bastard, from birth? I doubt it. Maybe, just maybe, he was a normal, happy little kid once.

I'm doing the world a favor by taking someone like me out of it. I don't want to know what I'm capable of. I don't want to know the first thrill of taking someone's life, that which old-man Levi is so fond of. I don't want to know how one's first killing equals that of the first time being with a woman.

Glancing at the gun, still clutched in my hand and resting in my lap, I see wet splatters glistening up at me. I've been crying and I don't know when the first tear fell. Alone now, there is no need or want for me to hide it. I just give myself over to it.

Eventually, I pull it together and stand up. At some point during my sobbing, I decided to make the mess in the bathroom since it will be easier to clean the tiled floor.

Part of me hates ending it all in a place where Ava and I were together. Still, another side finds the idea more acceptable and appealing than blasting my brains out all over the crucifix behind the pulpit—the only other tiled area in the chapel. I wedge the gun under my belt, slip the backpack over my arms, and take the longest walk ever down the center aisle toward the bathroom.

I haven't even gotten my hand on the bathroom doorknob yet when I hear the sound of the chapel doors' hinges squeaking open and a voice commanding, "Don't even think about it."

The voice is already known to me, but it sounds so full of contempt. I yank my hand away from the doorknob and spin around to find Christina kicking at a Turkey vulture so she can shut the chapel door. She's also pointing a gun at me.

I'm at a complete loss as to what's going on, or what I should do about it. "What are you doing? Where did you get that gun?"

"Put yours on the floor," she says.

"No."

"I said, put it on the damn floor!"

"I'm not doing it."

"Fine, then I'll shoot your kneecaps," Christina aims the gun at my legs, "so you can't move. Then I'll take your gun and go back to the front gate and shoot all your friends."

Had I actually been holding my own gun, I would consider the feasibility of disarming her first. As it stands, which doesn't look like I'll be doing for much longer based on how agitated she's getting with my hesitation, I relent and start to reach toward my belt.

"Two fingers, please . . . and slowly."

With thumb and forefinger, I slip the gun out and set it on the floor. "Why are you doing this?"

"Move." She jerks her head at somewhere behind me. "Over there by that table you fucked Ava on earlier. Walk backwards."

How the hell would Christina know about that? I can't imagine Gal would have told her. If not for my sake, he would never betray Ava like that. Holy shit! I remember now. I gave Christina access to my phone. She's probably been checking it all night. But how? She left her phone in the back of Gal's SUV. Or did she? I wasn't paying attention to *her*.

"Move your ass!"

"Okay."

I shuffle backward until my backside bumps into the front of the table.

"Sit down," she orders. I comply. "Put your hands flat on the floor." I comply again. "Good boy."

She walks over to my gun and stares hard at me while taking the risk of lowering her own to remove the mag from mine.

If only I'd known, I would have rushed her. I get a smug expression from her as she clears the bullet from the chamber. Still staring at me, gun redirected at my groin of all places, she flings the bullet filled mag toward the front door.

Only now does she seem satisfied enough to lower her weapon. "Slide your backpack over to me."

"I'll have to use my hands." I nod to my flattened palms.

"I don't recommend you get smart with me." She strolls over to me and stands there like a lord. Faster than I would have thought her capable of, Christina lands a precise punch to my face. Well, my blood finally spills, in the form and sound of a broken nose. "Lean forward and take off your bag, or I'll happily break both your arms and take it myself."

Again, I do as she demands. After watching her rifle through my backpack for a while, I ask, "What are you looking for?"

"Is there another mag in here?"

"No."

She tosses my empty gun inside the bag and kicks it back over to me. A half-smile forms on her face as she brandishes a plastic zip-tie from her pocket. "Put your right hand against the table leg." Since I take too long she reminds me, "Friends, Payton, they're still passed out from the drugs I spiked their water with. How absolutely boring they'd be for me to shoot. No fighting back, no protests. No begging for their lives."

Oh, my God. This bitch is crazy. A vision of how Ava, Gal, and Sunny looked before I left filters through my thoughts and I panic. "Have you already done it?"

"I wanted to, but I resisted the urge. Living leverage tends to have more sway." She fakes a worried expression. "At least I hope they're still breathing. I may have been too generous with the drugs I put in their water. I was in a hurry and it was dark . . . and technically, I'm not a pharmacist. Don't worry, there's still time. If only you would put your fucking wrist against the goddamn table leg like I told you to do!"

Loathe to put myself in the vulnerable position, I do it anyway and place my hand against the table leg. She secures the two together with the zip-tie and sits down in front of me.

"Feel better now?" The nasally sound of my voice robs me of the venom I had intended.

"You," Christina leans closer to look me squarely in the eyes, "are one messed up kid."

I already know that, but, seriously? "Yep, you would know," is all I give her and in doing so receive an open-handed slap to the face and the taste of my own blood trickling down from my broken nose.

Chapter Twenty-One

"What was it that you called me earlier in the Raynor Mausoleum?" She uses the barrel of the gun to wipe up some of the blood from my upper lip and smears it on my shirt.

"I believe it was bitch. Obviously, I hurt your feelings . . . bitch."

Christina kicks me in the groin with the heel of her boot. It hurts so much, I see stars and feel nauseous.

"Now I feel better," she says. "Those balls have seen a lot of action tonight, huh?"

"Is that what this is about? Are you jealous?" I have to admit, it sounds stupid having asked and I draw my knees up to my chest for protection.

"Oh, please, that's disgusting *and* insulting."

"Because I called you a bitch?" I'm yelling now.

"Nah." She shrugs. "I am a bitch. A good one, too." She takes her glasses off and tucks them into her front shirt pocket. "Useful things. I was worried you might recognize them as they're a similar product to the pen you've got there." Her gaze drifts to my front pocket. "Fortunately for me, Ava is a distraction for you. You're so like your father."

"What would you know about my father?"

I glimpse a flicker of raw hatred in her expression.

"I know he's my father, too."

Several silent seconds tick by, though it feels more like an hour or so. I'm trying to absorb what she just said. More importantly, I'm try making sense of it. I can't.

"What?"

Christina looks at me like I'm an idiot. "What part of Levi Raynor, Jr. is my father confused you? Is it the *how* part? Given your activities tonight, I feel certain you already know the how of it."

"My father has had a lot of affairs." I come to the only logical conclusion. "Are you the result of one of them?"

"Very good, Payton, you're not so stupid after all."

What I don't understand is why she seems to hate me so much. "Does he know about you?"

"No, but Levi, Sr. does. He's known since before I was born." My shock produces a cruel smile on her face. She leans in a little and adds, "He and I keep in touch, by the way."

"Why didn't your mother tell my . . . *our* father?"

The smug smile morphs into a sneer. "My mother was eighteen when he took advantage of her. He forgot to mention to her that he was married and had a kid, Wade. He disappeared without as much as a goodbye. She had to track him down to tell him about being pregnant with me and that's when she discovered he was married. Her mistake was that she tracked down the wrong Levi. It was our grandfather who informed her about his son already having a family. He convinced her to give me up for adoption to some personal friends of his, the Matthews. My mother vanished after the adoption. There is not one doubt in my mind that Levi Raynor, Sr. killed my mother."

"It wouldn't surprise me if he did, Christina. I told you before, he's evil." Something bothers me about this whole thing. "Why would you keep in touch with him?"

She looks right through me rather than at me and answers, "Revenge."

"You're gonna try to kill him?"

I'd wish her luck, but she's no match for the old man.

Her eyes refocus onto mine. "Maybe one day. For now, there's more torture in killing his hopes and dreams."

"You mean me?" I shake my head. "Had you not interrupted me, I was about to take care of that myself."

"I know, I've been hearing all your pathetic bullshit all night." She plucks a tiny earpiece out of her ear and shows it to me. "I couldn't believe how lucky I was when you gave me access to your data. You're such a moronic cliché."

Wow. I don't think I have ever been subjected to so many insults in so little time in my entire life. In a flat tone, I try appealing to her vengeful side, "Christina, let me save you the trouble. Walk out of here and let me finish what I planned to do."

"But I want that pleasure, just like it was a pleasure for me when I ran Wade off the road." She devotes every ounce of her attention now into watching my expression. "That's why I really got rid of him earlier tonight. I was afraid he would turn around and remember something. He did look at me right before his tires went off the road's shoulder."

I'm fluent in three languages and I can't nail down the right words in any one of them to accurately describe what is happening to me—what I'm feeling. It isn't good, it isn't bad, and yet it's both at the same time.

I can hear my heart pounding and I pretend it's hers and imagine how wonderful it would be if it stopped.

My internalized fantasies must be boring her because she stands and takes out a pocketknife from her backpack.

"I'm working in a tight time-frame here, Payton, and I have a lot of shit to do, so pay attention." She opens the knife and makes a slice across her palm without the slightest flinch of pain. After spreading some of her blood on my knees, the sides of my shorts, and my shirt, she smears plenty more on the pews and walls and the front door.

A quick survey of her painting skills apparently meets with her approval and she goes to the bathroom. I take full advantage of her stupidity. When she comes out, she's wrapping her hand in paper towels and eyeing me suspiciously.

"What are you doing?"

"Trying to shift positions," I answer. "My legs are falling asleep."

"Aw, poor baby." She fake tsks and sits down on the floor next to me. "I want to tell you about my plans while you're still breathing. Before I leave here, I'm going to put that mag," Christina points at the mag on the floor near the door, "back in our father's gun." She waves dismissively toward my backpack. "After I shoot you with it and wipe off my fingerprints, I'm going to put it in your dead hand."

"Will that make you feel vindicated, Christina?"

"Probably not as much as I'd like." She chuckles. "However, a murder-suicide scandal ought to shame the Raynor family name right out of decent society."

Despite the fact that I now know this whacked-out psycho killed my brother, I can't prevent the laughter that explodes past my lips. "Who the hell lied and told you Raynors were part of decent society?"

"Whatever," she says with a snarl. Good, I'm happy I rattled her cage a little. She nudges my ribs with her elbow, painfully. "Aren't you going to ask me who the murder victims are?"

I had been so keen to smash her image of the Raynor name being among Charleston's elitist upper echelon that, no, I didn't pay attention to the reference. But I am now and there is no way I'm so lucky that she means to off herself with me. I don't have to ask, I know where she's going with this. I'm quite certain she will tell me anyway, whether I ask or not.

All my life, nothing seems to ever work out for me. Not *really*. It's like these little good-luck moments will make things go my way from time to time. But nothing significant, and they're probably thrown at me just to keep me hopeful so I won't go off the deep end. Yet, here I am, my metaphorical feet inching forward on that diving board.

Why is there a dark cloud hanging over me? Did I do something in some past life that I'm being punished for in this one? If so, it hardly seems fair. Right now feels different, though. I'm on the cusp of something big. I can feel it like it's sneaking up on me from behind.

The only thing that stands in my way of knowing what it is would be for me to allow Christina to go through with her plans. I have a pretty good idea what it will lead to, and it still scares me. What choice do I have? None. I already made it. All I need is the moment to present itself for me to carry it out.

The universe doesn't smile at me. It smirks.

"Like you did, I stole this from home," she holds up the gun she's been pointing at me since coming in here, "right out of the Matthews' gun cabinet. I've been carrying it around in my backpack since last week. Of course, they kept it locked up like responsible parents, but I knew where they hid the key. Is that how you raided daddy's arsenal, knowing where he keeps the key?"

"Yeah."

I would almost regret having done it now, if I weren't so wrapped up in being thankful I had.

"Sort of cancels out the responsible-parent part, don't ya' think?" Her eyes seem vacant to me while they caress the barrel of the gun, like she's lost in a memory. "They're so worried about the outside getting in, they never think about the inside getting out."

There is no way in hell I'm getting into a weapons debate with this lunatic. I also don't want to get punched in the nuts again. "I guess."

"Know what I'm gonna do with it when I'm done with you? I'm going to put your finger prints all over it. Then I'm going to kill your friends and drop it near their bodies and walk out of Silentis and into a brand new life somewhere far away from here."

"You're not worried the investigators will suspect you were involved?" I'm already seeing the solution before hearing her answer. It looks like her blood all over me and the chapel.

"There's enough of my blood on you and in here for them to assume you killed me, too, even if they can't find my body. Based on your broken nose, they'll assume I put up a good fight." She laughs and sounds rather pleased with herself. "What a mystery it will be forever and ever. Where in Silentis did Payton Raynor put Christina's body?"

"The gates are locked. How are you going to walk out of here?"

She reaches into her pocket and pulls out a keychain. Two keys are attached to it: a smaller, newer-looking one—the kind that would open a padlock; and an older one that looks like it's been around a long time and would open a wrought iron gate that has been around for just as long. She dangles them in front of my face.

"Remember what I said? The Matthews are . . . well, were on the board of directors. These are the front gate keys."

"*Were*?"

"Yeah, they're dead now. I put two bullets from this gun into their heads before I left for school yesterday."

"Was that the first time you ever shot anyone?"

"Yeah."

"How did it feel?"

"It felt kind of good, actually." She stares at the keys for a second. "They knew what Levi did to my mother. I overheard them talking about it once when I started asking questions about my birth mother."

"You're a fantastic Raynor, Christina. Through and through."

"Probably." She leans in so close that all I see is what hatred and revenge looks like in someone's eyes. While running the barrel of the gun along my jawline, she asks, "But you're not, are you?"

I shift my body a little, as though to deliver my final words to her before she kills me. There's a look of mild amusement changing her expression, like she can't wait to hear what it is I have to say.

"Unfortunately, I think I am." I wait until I see the birth of a frown form on her forehead before continuing, "Never assume a fellow Raynor won't lie to you. You should have searched my pockets for a spare mag, and you shouldn't have turned your back to me. I could go on about how you made a mistake by leaving one my hands free and my backpack within easy reach, but I won't do that to you. I'd rather just get this over with and pretend like you never existed."

And then I shoot her. Twice. Once in the chest, to witness her shock and to see what a realized mistake looks like in someone else's eyes. Then, the second in the head to finish her off. Sadly, I hate how it feels only a little bit because I'm so deeply entrenched in *that* thrill. I think it's the giving in to being a Raynor that's the painful part. Of course, I could try convincing myself that it was either her or me.

I hadn't planned on killing Christina, but I did. It became necessary.

It's not over, though, and I know that. I still need to sell my soul to the devil. I'm pretty sure the price of ensuring that I won't go to jail, or to the nut-farm—and to secure the safety of Ava, Gal, and Sunny—will be me delivering myself over to that devil. Accept and embrace the Raynor life. The son of a bitch won.

I dig around in Christina's pockets for the knife and, yep, I find her cellphone. After cutting the zip-tie, I pick up her phone and search through her contacts. He answers on the second ring, "Yes, Christina."

"Nope, it's Payton," I say to old man Raynor. "Christina's dead, I made sure of it when I put the second bullet in her head." His diplomatic silence answers all my questions. "How 'bout we renegotiate?"

Nothing at first, then his evil laughter comes through and fills the chapel. "Are you sure, boy?"

"Yes. It's your choice, old man. We can either come to an agreement, or I can kill you when you least expect it." It's a threat meant to make him experience a sliver of fear. I'm not sure if he is capable of fear, but I am sure of one thing—I will live long enough to watch this monster take his last breath.

His laughter assaults the holy sanctuary again before it fades. I sense that what little hope there was for benevolence is slipping away from me now. It is a painful death and I hear it moving in rhythm with the sound of, not Taps, but with Mrs. White's hummed goodbye-lullaby to her baby.

I almost wish he would challenge me. There are plenty of bullets left in this gun and I only need one if I get a whiff of his refusal to help me. He won't, though, and he and I both know it. I'm a Raynor, through and through, and I just proved it to him and to myself. Not only have I joined the ranks of Raynors who kill, but I killed another Raynor and look forward to doing it again.

"Very good, Payton. It's about time. So, tell me where you are so I can get this mess cleaned up."

ACKNOWLEDGMENTS

Friends and family who helped make it possible, who put with all my:

- Crap.
- Angst.
- Insecurities.
- Typos, missing words, and wtfs.
- Endless questions, some of which I still have.
- Fart jokes.
-   (fill in the blank)   .

Anna Wiggins, Patrick Harwood, Pamela Mather, Moonchild, Laura McConnell, Matthew Keeley, Christina Stanfill, Propwash Gary, every cemetery in Charleston (~~some more than others~~ one in particular), dead people (sorry for stepping on your graves), Charleston (you know I love you, right?), the glorious internet, Bonnie Cliff (Merci!), Frank Grant, the late Ted Ashton Phillips, Jr., so many agents (you know I love you, right?), Magali Fréchette, and myself…for wanting it bad enough and for doing it my way.

…And last, but never least:

Dear Mom,
This is my second chance to tell you that,
You were taken from me too soon.
I think about you all the time.
I miss you every single day.
I love you…always.